"Too bad you're saving yourself for your husband."

Shock at Tony's unexpected remark brought Erin out of her passion-induced daze. "What?"

"While I can admire your position," he continued smoothly, "it's not one that works to my benefit. Bedding you would be like promising commitment. So run into the house, little girl, before I change my mind."

"You're insufferable!" Erin cried. "You seem to think that the only thing standing between you and me sleeping together is your reluctance. I might have something to say about it, you know."

Tony smiled at her outburst. "Honey, if I wanted, I could have you in my bed before you could reel off the names of your brothers."

"Of all the egotistical males!" Erin fumed. Never mind that he was right.

Jeanne Allan, born and raised in Nebraska, lived there until she married a United States Air Force lieutenant. More than a dozen moves have taken them to Germany and ten different states. Between moves Jeanne spends time as a seasoned volunteer, and makes all kinds of crafts including stained-glass windows. With their two teenage children she enjoys nature walks, bird-watching and photography at their cabin in the Colorado mountains. She has always liked to write, but says her husband bullied her into writing her first romance novel.

Books by Jeanne Allan

HARLEQUIN ROMANCE
2665—PETER'S SISTER
2845—WHEN LOVE FLIES BY
2875—THE WAITING HEART

Don't miss any of our special offers. Write to us at the following address for information on our newest releases.

Harlequin Reader Service
901 Fuhrmann Blvd., P.O. Box 1397, Buffalo, NY 14240
Canadian address: P.O. Box 603,
Fort Erie, Ont. L2A 5X3

The Game Is Love

Jeanne Allan

Harlequin Books

TORONTO • NEW YORK • LONDON
AMSTERDAM • PARIS • SYDNEY • HAMBURG
STOCKHOLM • ATHENS • TOKYO • MILAN

Original hardcover edition published in 1987
by Mills & Boon Limited

ISBN 0-373-02899-7

Harlequin Romance first edition April 1988

CHAPTER ONE

ERIN CASSIDY leaned over the work bench, her lower lip caught between her teeth, as she concentrated on cutting a difficult inside curve from the expensive piece of red glass. The warm April afternoon had seduced her into opening the workshop windows, and now the urgent wailing of an ambulance set her nerves on edge as she grasped the glass carefully, one thumb on either side of the scored line, and quickly rotated her wrists. The glass parted perfectly, and Erin let out the breath she had been unconsciously holding. The siren died away leaving a peaceful stillness in the neighbourhood. A stillness broken almost immediately by a metallic-sounding crash. In the sudden silence that resulted, the tinkling of broken glass echoed in Erin's head.

Not the lavender glass! The words tumbled prayerfully over and over again in her mind as she rushed out of the studio door and down the steep outside staircase. A dark blue sports car sat with its nose inelegantly pushed up against a shattered wooden crate. Colourful shards of glass glittered in the April sunshine. The precious, long-awaited lavender glass—reduced to scraps.

'You idiot,' she shrieked, 'how could you do such a stupid thing?' Belatedly she noticed the girl shrinking against the back of the driver's seat, her teenage face registering shocked dismay. The wobbling of the girl's lower lip penetrated Erin's anger, and her conscience stabbed at her.

Before she could apologise for her unbridled outburst, a man erupted from the passenger side of the car. 'Who do you think you're calling an idiot?' he shouted. 'Only an idiot would leave something like this sitting in the middle of the driveway.'

Erin welcomed a target more appropriate for venting her anger. 'It's my driveway and I can put whatever I damn well please in it,' she shouted back.

The man stalked around the back of the car to where Erin stood with clenched fists rammed against her hips. 'Don't shout at me,' he said coldly, thrusting his square-cut face down into hers.

Erin gaped at him in angered astonishment before jabbing a stiff finger against his chest. 'Listen you, whoever you are, I'll shout if I want to. Do you know what you've done?' She chose to ignore the fact that he hadn't been driving.

'The crate should never have been left here,' he repeated in a tight, angry voice, swatting her finger aside as if it were a fly.

Suddenly Erin was aware of the man's size as he loomed ominously over her, and she involuntarily moved back a step. He kept pace with her, forcing her back up against the shattered crate. The gleam of satisfaction in his eyes at her small display of fear stiffened her spine. 'Since it's all your fault, I'll expect you to pay for the damage,' she said coldly.

'How much?'

Tempted to spit out a gargantuan total, Erin said instead, 'I'll have to take an inventory before I can assess the damage you've done. Leave your name and address, and I'll send you a bill.'

'No doubt inflating the total,' he sneered. 'Since your crate scratched my car, perhaps I ought to send you the bill for a new paint job.'

'My glass wasn't moving, your car was!' she cried angrily.

'Where are your witnesses?' he asked nastily.

Erin gasped out loud at his outrageous question. 'Do you mean to stand there and deny that this whole mess is your fault?'

'It's not Tony's fault. It's mine.' The woebegone voice came from the forgotten driver. 'I just got my learner's permit and I begged Tony to let me drive his car.' A small sob escaped her lips. 'I promised him that I'd be so careful.'

'It's not your fault,' Erin consoled the girl. 'He had no business letting a beginner drive a car like this.'

'He had to,' the driver wailed. 'I pestered him and pestered him. Now I'll have a blot on my driving record, and my parents will have a fit, and I'll be ancient before I ever get to drive again.'

Erin dug deep into the pockets of her grimy jeans until she found a clean tissue. She handed it to the girl who was becoming awash with tears. 'Wipe your face,' she commanded briskly. 'There's no need for us to bother the police over a little mishap like this. I'm sure we can work something out between us.'

'What did you have in mind? Blackmail?'

Erin had forgotten the man who leaned back against his car, icicle-blue eyes regarding her with derision. Blond, wavy hair, tousled from the breezy ride, carelessly framed a handsome, rugged face. Lips twisted with scorn. Erin hesitated, two emotions warring within her. Sympathy for the young driver pushed her to play down the accident, but the arrogance of the girl's companion and his attempt to place the entire blame for the accident on Erin made her blood boil. 'I think it would be better if we discussed this at a later date when your sense of justice is not being blocked by emotion,' Erin said, condescension coating her every word.

His eyes narrowed. 'What a clever ploy to get to see me again.'

Erin's mouth dropped open. 'How dare you insinuate I have any personal interest in you? Just give me a name and address where I can send the bill because all I want from you is the money for the damage.'

Angrily he whipped his wallet from a back pocket and ripped out a business card, practically throwing it at Erin. She stuck it in her pocket without looking at it.

'Don't you know who Tony is?' the girl behind the wheel asked in startled surprise.

'Should I?'

'He's Tony Hart.'

'Good for him.'

'I can't believe you don't know Tony. His picture is always in the newspapers,' the girl persisted.

'I don't read the police reports,' Erin said smoothly.

The man uttered a sharp, barking laugh. 'Move over, Allie. I'll drive home.'

The girl started to protest, but the look on the man's face silenced her and she swiftly complied. The car backed smoothly out of the driveway, stopping cautiously at the street before roaring away.

Hands thrust deep in her pockets, Erin watched them leave, fighting the angry tears of frustration which threatened at this latest disaster. The stained-glass window commissioned by Mrs Filmore had been an unexpected plum dropped in her lap, but then one setback after another had followed. The unusual lavender European glass that she had selected for the window was not available locally, and when she had finally located a New York company that handled it, they had been out of stock and had to order some more. With each delay, Mrs Filmore had grown more and more impatient. Erin cringed at the thought of calling her client and explaining this further delay. Mrs Filmore was the one woman she had no desire to displease. This commission was supposed to be Erin's big break. Ever since she had been forced to relocate in Denver, getting her stained-glass business off the ground had been a long, continuous struggle. Mrs Filmore lived in a very exclusive development south of Denver, and Erin had great hopes that a satisfied customer in that area would lead to a number of high-priced commissions. Unfortunately, Mrs Filmore had already voiced the opinion that perhaps she should have gone to an established firm so that she might have received her window sooner.

Erin turned her back on the shattered crate and, detouring around a large lilac bush, walked to the old stone wall that separated the Cassidy yard from Sloan Park. Elbows on the wall, she ignored the chill pine-scented breeze that swirled around her shoulders and whipped up small white caps on the lake. Even Mother Nature's diversified spring palette—the various greens of new growth, the fiery red breast of a house finch, the cerulean sky and the deep purple mountain range in the background—failed to raise her depressed spirits. She envied the happy, carefree children romping on the playground. A year ago, filled with promise for the future, she had been that happy. Then her mother had unexpectedly suffered a stroke, and with one swift wave of her wand, fate had altered Erin's life. She had immediately flown back from Phoenix where she had been working for a large firm that specialised in church and commercial stained-glass. Her stay was meant to be temporary, but it had quickly become apparent that her mother's recovery would be slow and that Erin was needed at home. She had flown back to Arizona, quit her job, said sad farewells and shipped all her belongings home to Denver. As Mrs Cassidy improved, it had been her idea that the empty apartment over their garage could be turned into a workshop for Erin.

The year hadn't been easy. First worry over her mother's condition, and then the struggle to establish herself. Black moments of despair and self-pity were all too frequent in the beginning. But just when life seemed darkest, the sight of her mother fighting back from her stroke shamed Erin and aroused her fighting spirit. Slowly, gradually, she acquired customers, relying exclusively on word of mouth. Modest success appeared to be within her grasp. Until today. Mrs Filmore was going to be furious.

Erin heard her name called and looked up. Nicky was jogging around the lake towards her, disturbing a small flock of Canada geese that honked and flapped their wings at his intrusion before waddling towards the water, a single grackle keeping pace on their flank. Evading the geese, Nicky hurdled the stone wall, barely missing a vivid yellow daffodil bed.

He grinned unrepentantly at Erin's look of reproof. 'You'll never guess who I just saw driving through the park.'

Erin smiled fondly at her youngest brother. Fifteen years old, Nicky bubbled over with youthful exuberance. 'Who?'

'Tony Hart.'

Erin gave him a blank stare.

'Tony Hart,' Nicky repeated impatiently. 'You know. The quarterback for the Denver Explorers football team. Gosh, I wonder what he was doing in our neighbourhood.'

'Trying to put me out of business,' Erin explained drily, thumbing in the direction of the busted crate.

'Tony Hart did that? He was here? Wait until I tell the guys. Tony Hart in my yard. And I wasn't here,' he wailed in anguish. 'Did you get his autograph?'

'Not yet, but I better. On a nice, big, fat cheque.'

'You'd make him pay for this little accident? Tony Hart?'

'Quit saying "Tony Hart" as if he's some kind of god,' Erin said in disgust.

'He practically is! The Explorers were in the league basement until they traded for Tony a couple years ago. If you didn't spend so much time in art museums, your brain wouldn't have turned to mush, and you'd know what was going on in the world today.'

'I hardly think following the exploits of a losing football team is paying attention to world news.'

'It is if you live in Denver,' Nicky pointed out. 'Besides, that's the whole point. With Tony, the Explorers aren't losing any more. They made the play-offs this year, and even though they lost in the first round, everyone expects them to go a lot farther next year.'

'You mean to tell me that one man made that much difference?' Erin asked sceptically.

'Not just any man. Tony Hart. He's not only got one of the greatest arms since Namath, he's a leader. He expects the other guys to give a hundred and ten per cent, and because he gives it himself, they do. He's always doing something for charity, especially for kids. Drugs are his pet hate, and he's real involved fighting them.'

'Does he walk on water, too?'

'Make fun if you want, Erin, but Tony Hart's a real asset to his team and his community. He's the stuff of heroes, a man that kids can look up to without fear of disillusionment. And in today's world, we need heroes like Tony.'

'These words from Nicholas Cassidy? The lad whose English teacher said he had trouble putting together enough words to make a complete sentence?'

Nicky blushed. 'There was a big spread about him a few weeks ago in one of my sports magazines. What was Tony doing in our driveway?'

'I told you. Running over my crate of glass.'

'C'mon, Erin. He must have had some reason for turning in here. Didn't he tell you?'

'He was too busy blaming me for the scratches on his precious car to say anything else.'

'You scratched his Porsche?' Nicky asked in horror. 'You know how much a car like that costs?'

'Nicky!' Erin screeched.

'Why'd you leave that crate in the middle of the driveway anyway? That's pretty dumb.'

'I did not leave it in the middle of the driveway. The man who delivered it took one look at those steep stairs, mumbled something about union regulations, and dumped the crate right where you see it. Did you expect me to haul it upstairs all by myself? I was waiting for you and Dad to come home. Of course, there's no problem now. I'll just get a broom and dustpan.'

'Ah, it's not that bad. I'll bet there's still some pretty good-size pieces in there.' He thumped the side of the crate. An ominous tinkle of glass from within answered him. 'Oops.' He grimaced apologetically at Erin.

She glared back at him. 'There's not one piece of lavender glass left big enough for Mrs Filmore's window.'

'She'll understand. It's not as if it's your fault.'

'Maybe you're right,' Erin said hopefully. 'After all the trips I've made to her home, not to mention all the patterns I drew before she was satisfied, she wouldn't fire me now just because of a small delay.'

Erin slammed down the phone. Mrs Filmore certainly would fire Erin because of a small delay. Mr Filmore had told his wife all along that not dealing with a well known firm was a mistake. Mrs Filmore should have listened to her husband right from the beginning.

A copy of the inventory for the broken glass lay on the work bench in front of Erin. She wished she had had the nerve to charge Tony Hart for business lost as well as the actual cost of the broken glass. He could certainly afford it better than she could. Apparently he was paid a great deal of money for playing a game.

One day while Nicky was in school Erin sneaked into his room and read the magazine article about the great Tony Hart. She was curious about the man who could create such an unfavourable impression on her and at the same time be the saint that Nicky spoke about. Of course, Nicky would overlook triple homicide since the man was a star football player. Because Tony Hart's love for his close-knit family was one of many saintly virtues that the magazine had extolled with nauseating detail, Erin knew that the driver of the car had been his younger sister, Allie.

The one thing that Nicky hadn't mentioned was that the quarterback's philanthropic reputation was matched only by his reputation among the ladies. Tony Hart, the magazine pointed out, was a connoisseur when it came to beautiful women. Asked about his playboy image, the quarterback had laughed and said the only reason for a man to get married was to have someone to take care of his dog while he was on the road. All the pretty words about the multiple charities that Tony Hart gave his time and energies to paled in Erin's mind beside that remark. It confirmed her belief that the man who was at least partially responsible for the accident—after all, he did allow his sister to drive his sports car—was a man of little substance with an over-inflated ego.

At least she now knew why he had been in her driveway in the first place. The reason was sitting against the far wall of her studio. An enormous stained-glass window of a football player running with the ball, hand out to fend off any attackers. The player depicted was Neal Roberts, a running back on the Denver Explorers, the same team that Tony Hart played for.

Erin had met Merry Roberts, Neal's wife, in front of the quilts on exhibit at the Denver Art Museum. The two women had struck up a casual conversation that had continued over lunch and turned out to be the beginning of a new and warm friendship. When Merry had broached the idea of a window celebrating her husband's athletic prowess, Erin had been pleased to come up with a design. The finished window was a surprise, to be given to Neal at his birthday party. Merry had asked Tony to stop by Erin's shop and discuss the logistics of transporting the window to the Robertses' house. After Tony's abortive trip, Merry had phoned Erin in remorse. Tony had been furious, Allie was still crying and she, Merry, felt terrible about the damage to Erin's glass. It had finally been settled that Erin would come early to the party, carefully transporting the window in the back of her father's station wagon.

Driving south on Parker Road the evening of Merry's party, heavy traffic on the old highway forced Erin to concentrate on her driving. Brand new housing developments crowding out small farms gave evidence that modern transportation was transforming Parker from a sleepy little settlement that had grown up around a stage stop in the late 1800s to a dormitory community for present-day Denver. The Robertses lived in an exclusive new area just south of Parker, and Erin hoped that at least some of their friends and neighbours might be interested in commissioning her to make windows for their homes. Now that the Filmore commission was lost it was more important than ever that Erin develop and pursue other avenues. She couldn't afford to miss this party, even if she did have to go alone.

Merry had told her she might bring an escort, and Erin had immediately invited Martin Thomas, an account executive with a large advertising firm in Denver. She had been dating Martin for several months now, and had hoped that he would accompany her. Unfortunately, Martin hated contact sports, especially football. Even more than football, Martin detested football players. There was no way that he was going to ruin an entire evening standing around listening to a bunch of dumb jocks brag about their silly feats. Since Erin shared his sentiments, she couldn't blame him for rejecting her invitation. Still, she told herself wistfully, as she slowed down for the entrance to the housing area, Martin would have provided her with moral support.

Merry's two small sons gave her no opportunity to indulge in self-pity. As soon as she arrived at the Robertses' house, seeing Merry harassed by last-minute details, Erin willingly went with the boys up to their enormous playroom to keep them out of their mother's way. Erin suggested reading a story, but the boys clamoured to play ball, and soon she was begging for a short rest. 'I'm a lot older than you guys, you know.'

'You're getting better,' Adam, the oldest child, said encouragingly. 'You even caught the ball once.' He laughed in delight when Erin grabbed for him and missed.

'Didn't you ever play football when you were a kid?' Davy asked.

'Nope. My mother had five boys and she wanted a girl who was all girl. I had lots of dolls, pink dresses, dance lessons and pretty books. But I never had a ball.'

'I'm sorry,' Davy said seriously.

'You are not,' Erin joked. 'Then you couldn't win so easily. Come on. Play ball!' She tossed the foam football to Adam, but her aim was off, and it sailed way over his head.

Adam giggled. 'I think you need someone else on your team.'

'How about me?' The deep voice from the doorway startled Erin.

'Tony, Tony!' The two small boys rushed to the tall man leaning in the open doorway. He straightened up just as the first whirlwind hit, Davy climbing the football player as if he were a tree. Adam had to be content with twining his arms about the long, muscled legs.

'Hi, guys. Did I hear Adam say that you were looking for a football player to help out your pretty friend?' He gave Erin a slow, sensuous smile, one loaded with masculine charm and sex appeal.

No wonder he's such a success with the ladies, Erin thought in amused contempt. The quarterback was dressed in a snug-fitting blue shirt that matched his blue eyes and emphasised his muscled torso. A thin gold chain around his neck drew attention to the tanned column of skin exposed by the open-collared shirt. Erin's gaze was drawn to the small indentation that vertically bisected his square-cut chin. That must drive his lady friends wild.

A sudden, intriguing realisation turned her thoughts. Tony Hart had no idea who she was. He never would have smiled like that if he had recognised her. A mischievous imp whispered in Erin's ear that it would be fun to string along this egotistical male who thought that he was God's gift to womankind. She owed him, oh, how she owed him, for the damage done to her business. With five brothers, she knew enough about males to know that he wouldn't have forgiven her for his having come off second-best at their last encounter. What a shocking blow it would be to him to discover that he was making a fool of himself over the one woman that he wanted nothing to do with. She gave

him a quick, flirtatious look, and then turned away,
her lips half curved in promise.

His eyes gleamed with satisfaction before he set
Davy down. 'Well, will I do?'

'Yeah, yeah!' Adam jumped up and down.

'I'll have to change my name,' Davy said sadly.
Tony looked down at the small boy in puzzlement. 'Why?'

''Cuz I'm you. Tony Hart. And Adam is Jim
McMahon.'

'Going over to the opposition, are you?' Tony
teased the small boy. He looked over at Erin. 'And
you are?'

Quickly, before the boys could divulge her real
name, Erin spoke up, 'Alex Karras.'

'A Karras fan? You can't be that old,' Tony said.

Erin wrinkled up her nose. 'I'm not much
interested in football. Or football players,' she said
smoothly. Ignoring the stunned look on this particular player's face, she added, 'I've seen Alex
Karras on TV and his was the only name I could
think of.'

'He's an actor, not a football player, isn't he,
Tony?' Adam asked in disgust.

'Today, maybe. But in his day, he was one of the
best.' Seeing that Adam was prepared to argue,
Tony grabbed the ball from Erin and tossed it to
the small boy.

And the game was on. Erin and Adam against
Tony and Davy.

It didn't take Erin three minutes to realise that
Tony Hart was playing the game on two levels.
Genuinely interested in the children, he was a born
coach, mixing unstinting praise with clear in-
struction. The boys clearly adored him and copied
his every move. At the same time, he missed no
opportunity to touch Erin, put his arm around her

shoulders to demonstrate a throw or give her one of his sensuous smiles.

Erin's hand itched to slap him, but that would interfere with her plans. Instead she pretended to be amused by his tactics. Living with five brothers had taught her that nothing so deflated the male ego as being laughed at. When Tony brought his face close to hers, supposedly to block for Davy, she made sure that he noticed lips quivering in an effort not to laugh. He eyed her thoughtfully, but said nothing. The next time she had the ball, he managed to manoeuvre her into a corner, his body brushing against hers as he pretended to tackle her. Blue eyes smouldered as he slowly bent his head.

'What are you doing, Tony?' Adam asked. 'You let her go or you're gonna get a penalty for holding.'

Erin giggled under her breath, just loud enough to reach Tony's ears. He stiffened. Good, thought Erin. That should teach him that not every woman is dying to fall into his arms. She stepped around his body and threw the ball to Adam. Unfortunately it fell way short, right into Davy's hands. With a loud crow of delight, the small boy ran towards Tony who swept him up on his shoulders and raced with him to the chairs that indicated the goal line.

'Touchdown!' Davy shouted. 'We won.'

'I want to see an instant replay,' Erin demanded.

Tony grinned. 'Sore loser.' His eyes narrowed in speculation. 'When a team wins the Super Bowl, each player gets a ring. What do we get for winning this game? How 'bout a kiss?'

'Yuk,' Davy said, screwing up his face in distaste. 'I'd rather have a cookie.'

Erin laughed out loud. 'The team captain speaks. Besides,' she said huffily, 'Alex Karras does not kiss the team that defeated him.'

'Of course, now that the game is over, you don't have to be Karras any more. You can be?' His voice lifted in interrogation.

Before Erin was forced to evade his question, Merry entered the room with a swirl of ruffles. 'Here you two are. Tony, Jennifer is looking all over for you, and she's starting to get annoyed. Besides, I want to unveil the window now. I can't wait any longer to see the look on Neal's face.' She looked from one to the other with puzzled eyes. 'You two seem to be getting along well.'

Before Merry could divulge her identity, Erin spoke up. 'Don't be misled by appearances. McMahon and Karras just lost the big game, and we don't take defeat lightly. Right, McMahon?' She tousled Adam's hair.

'Right, Karras,' Adam answered stoutly.

Realisation dawned on Merry's face. Erin hoped it wasn't as obvious to Tony as it was to her.

Merry turned to Tony. 'I'll wait while, er, Karras combs her hair. She looks like she's been playing football.'

Davy giggled. 'She has, Mommy.'

Merry rolled her eyes back in her head. 'You two run along to the kitchen and have a snack and then it's bedtime for you. As for you, Tony, you'd better get back to the party before Jennifer pitches a fit.'

Tony laughed. 'I don't think that Jennifer can come close to matching your Miss Cassidy when it comes to throwing a tantrum. She's the one you need to keep an eye on.' With a flip of his hand, he disappeared out of the door behind the boys.

'I take it Tony doesn't know who you are,' Merry said drily.

'That's right,' Erin said. 'I can hardly wait to see the look on his face when he figures it out.'

Merry frowned. 'I don't understand why he didn't recognise you.'

'I don't normally dress like this for work.' Erin looked down at the dark lavender camisole top. 'I'd be covered with band-aids if I did. Not to mention that I was wearing safety goggles that cover most of my face, and my hair was hidden under an old ragged scarf. I thought he might recognise my voice, but he was too busy flirting to even think about the other day.'

'Flirting?' Merry asked with obvious casualness.

Erin lightly patted her nose with powder, hoping to erase the shine created from such strenuous exercise. Her eyes locked with Merry's in the mirror. 'Tony Hart is the worst come-on artist I've ever encountered.'

Merry carefully inspected her buffed nails. 'I take it you're not the least interested.'

'Not the least,' Erin confirmed.

'Merry! Where's the extra ice?' Neal's voice bellowed up the stairs.

'Men! They're helpless.' Half running, Merry left.

Alone, Erin inspected her image in the mirror. No question but that she presented quite a different picture tonight from the other day. Her black wavy hair was tousled from the game, with small damp tendrils curling attractively about her face. Her father always kidded her about her bright blue eyes, calling her a true Irish lass, even though she was a fifth-generation American. He also claimed that his grandmother had been one of the most beautiful women in Colorado in her younger days, a statement that few disputed. Erin was a carbon copy of her. Remembering a picture of her ancestor dressed in high-necked blouse and long, puffed sleeves, Erin wondered what she would have thought of the more revealing styles of today. Her own lavender outfit exposed creamy white shoulders, while the silky fabric of the trousers outlined her form and emphasised her long legs. In her great-grandmother's day, women weren't even supposed to know they had legs, much less use them to attract a man's eye. Tony Hart had certainly approved of what she was wearing. Not that she cared. Erin outlined her lips in a deep rose. She had better hurry down so that Merry could unveil the window and introduce Erin as the artist. The surprise on Tony Hart's face was one sight she didn't want to miss.

All the guests were gathered together out on the wide wooden deck. Some were wondering what was going on, while others smugly admitted that they were in the know. Neal was clowning around, professing total ignorance, oblivious to the fact that it was his birthday.

Tony Hart materialised at Erin's side.

'Jennifer been appeased?' she asked mockingly.

Tony nodded, but his attention was clearly elsewhere as he surveyed the area, a slight frown marring his brow.

'Problem?'

'Merry said that she wouldn't unveil the window until that Cassidy woman arrived, and I was just wondering where she is. Merry had a hard enough time herding everyone out here. If something doesn't happen soon, the crowd will be wandering back inside to the bar and the buffet.'

Erin swallowed a giggle. 'It looks like Merry is ready now.'

The night went black as all the outside floodlights were turned off. Tony took advantage of the darkness to move closer to Erin. She ignored the flirtatious nonsense that he whispered in her ear, intent on the presentation of her window. The only way to do justice to the gleaming jewel colours of the glass was to have light behind it, a fact that had caused Erin and Merry no end of trouble as they planned this evening. Finally Erin had hit upon the idea of everyone going outside in the dark and switching on the lights inside the house behind the window.

Having gained everyone's attention, Merry made a clever little speech about Neal's birthday. Then she banged on the glass behind her and the curtains were opened. There was a moment of silence followed by a low hum of appreciation from the audience.

Neal grabbed his wife's hand and gave her a hearty kiss to wild applause.

Slightly dishevelled, Merry stepped out of his arms. 'I'd like to introduce the artist, if she'll step up here.'

'I wonder where the old battle-axe is,' Tony whispered in Erin's ear.

'Right here,' she said, smiling sweetly into his face.

Tony looked as if he had been belted in the stomach. Enjoying his reaction, Erin barely heard Merry's words of praise.

As far as Erin was concerned, the party was an immense success. The window she had designed for the Robertses was widely admired, and at least half a dozen people took her name and phone number, hopefully to contact her later. She felt giddy with triumph. Not even Tony Hart's scowling face from across the room dampened her pleasure. If anything, the knowledge that she had bested him added something to her evening. Whoever said revenge was sweet was right on target.

CHAPTER TWO

'Who would have guessed that the face and body of an angel harboured the soul of a witch.' Tony Hart stood beside her, sipping from a frosted glass.

'Not you, that's for sure.' Erin smiled triumphantly up into his darkened eyes.

'Did you get my cheque?'

'Yes.'

'Yes? Just yes? Not, yes, thank you?'

'Why should I thank you? You were only paying what you owed me,' Erin flashed.

'The bill seemed rather high to me,' Tony said coolly.

'High!' Erin repeated incredulously. 'You're lucky I only charged you for the broken glass. You have no idea how much potential business I lost because of that crash.'

Tony looked sceptical. 'Allie said you told her over the phone that the glass was easily replaced and that the crash caused you no problems.'

Erin avoided his gaze. 'She felt bad enough.' There was no reason for him to know that Erin had felt sorry for his teenage sister.

Tony gave her a quizzical look. 'Don't tell me that the icy Miss Cassidy has a melting heart.'

'At least I have a heart, which is more than can be said about you.'

'And what's that supposed to mean?'

'Denver's most elusive bachelor, I believe today's paper dubbed you. Tony Hart. Love 'em and leave 'em Hart. Women fling their hearts before him, but he never loses his. Maybe because the only heart he has is his name.'

'I'm flattered you were interested enough in me to read that trash.'

'I wasn't,' Erin snapped. 'My little brother Nicky has this disgusting habit of reading the paper to me over the breakfast table, and this morning he insisted on reading that article to me.'

'Actually it wasn't as bad as I anticipated,' he said. 'Sally Powers made a play for me at a party a while back, and I wasn't interested. It wasn't until later that I discovered that she was a reporter.'

A whimsical grin tilted one corner of his mouth, precipitating an unwelcome fluttering in the pit of Erin's stomach, and she forced herself to concentrate on what he had said. 'In which case you would have been interested, I suppose.'

'No, but I might have sugar-coated the no a little better.'

'That's sickening.' The flutter was gone.

Tony shrugged. 'No, that's life. My life. I'm in the entertainment business, and it doesn't pay to upset my fans. Besides, I don't like kids like your brother reading and believing that stuff.'

'Don't worry,' Erin said sweetly. 'I assured Nicky that it couldn't possibly be true. That you were too nasty to be irresistible to women. I said you probably told the reporter that to build up your fan club.'

Unexpectedly a flash of amusement crossed his face and crinkled up the corners of his eyes, lending a sensuous charm to his countenance. Erin felt her stomach flip-flop again. 'Allie tried to tell me how nice you were to her on the phone when she called to apologise,' he added lazily. 'I didn't believe her.

Thought she was just trying to downplay the accident so I wouldn't tell our folks.'

Erin ignored the insult. 'Did you tell them?'

'You kidding? And have Allie pass along all she knows about me?' His eyes opened wide in pretended horror.

Erin laughed unwillingly. The man undeniably had charm, but he could go and exercise it on some other female. A tall, black man walked up to Tony with a quip that Jennifer was looking for him, and Erin took advantage of the interruption to drift away.

An hour later Tony cornered her again. 'How about making a window for me?' he asked.

Erin raised a brow in amused interrogation. Really. This man was unbelievable. Apparently he wasn't accustomed to women who refused to worship at his feet. Having failed with the obvious tactic, he was switching to one he was sure she would fall for. Pretending that he wanted a window. She looked him coolly in the face. 'No.'

'No?' he asked in disbelief.

'I'm too busy.'

'I guess that was just a lie about all the potential business you lost because of the crash,' he needled her.

'It was not.'

'Well then? Think of all the advantages to you if I commission you to design a window for me. I can sit in front of it to be photographed during all my interviews, and the phones will ring off the wall wanting to know who the artist is.'

Erin bit her lip. There was a certain amount of truth to what he said. If he really did intend to have her make him a window, that was. How could she be sure it wasn't just a new version of the 'come

up and see my etchings' routine? A thought occurred to her. 'I enjoyed making the window for
Neal, but I'm not sure that I want to be known as
the lady who does football players.'

'I was thinking more along the lines of a naked
lady.'

'Then you can forget it,' Erin said heatedly. 'If
you want naked ladies, I'm sure some of your
female companions would be more than happy to
oblige.'

'In bed, of course.' A mocking smile said he was
being deliberately provocative.

'I don't do naked women.'

'I'm sure naked isn't your style,' he smoothly
agreed.

Erin eyed him suspiciously. 'And what is that
remark supposed to mean? If you're trying to challenge me into . . .' She swallowed the rest of the sentence—'your bed'.

'You're so quick to misjudge me,' he said in an
aggrieved voice, a look of injured innocence on his
face which didn't fool Erin for a minute. 'We are
talking about windows, aren't we?'

Erin was beginning to understand why this man
was so heralded on the football field as a great
strategist. He was certainly manoeuvring her into
a corner. She didn't believe that he really wanted
a window, but his comments were all so smooth
that there was nothing to grab hold of to prove her
suspicions. On the one hand, she needed the
business, and he wasn't a connection that she could
cavalierly dismiss. Neither could she confess her
thoughts out loud. After her earlier remarks about
his reputation that the ladies couldn't leave him
alone, he would love to turn her own words against
her. To accuse him of pursuing her was the same

as saying that she thought she was irresistible to the opposite sex. The same charge she had levelled against him. Only in her case it wasn't true. She merely thought that her lack of interest intrigued and challenged him. Convincing Tony Hart that she wasn't interested in him might prove to be a task beyond her capabilities. His attitude about the accident, and his lack of contrition, proved his tunnel vision. If only she didn't need the business. She gnawed indecisively on her lower lip.

'If you discourage all your customers like this you're going to starve to death,' Tony chided her.

Erin made up her mind. 'Strictly business?'

'Of course, what else?' He pretended astonishment. 'Don't tell me you think I'm making a pass at you?' The innocent look on his face warred with the satisfaction that shone in his eyes.

Already Erin regretted her decision. Over Tony's shoulder she could see a tall brunette watching them. As the woman realised that Erin saw her she made beckoning motions with her hand. 'I think you're being paged.'

Tony glanced over his shoulder. 'That's just Jennifer. She'll wait.'

'Of course she will,' Erin smoothly agreed. 'After all, you're the great Tony Hart and she's ... just Jennifer.'

Giving her a dirty look, Tony turned on his heel and made his way across the crowded room to the brunette's side. Erin watched in amused disgust as Jennifer's bright red lips pouted up at Tony, and it didn't surprise her when, after only a few words from Tony, the woman's face was wreathed with smiles. Tony had obviously won her over. One almost had to admire a man who could spend an entire evening chasing after one woman and at the same time keep a second one content.

'Rampant masculinity.'

Erin turned swiftly at the voice in her ear.

Merry stood there smiling at her. 'There's a kind of leashed power that athletes seem to exude. It translates directly into sexual appeal.'

'Oh ho, so that's what you saw in Neal,' Erin teased.

'Yup,' Merry complacently agreed, before giggling, a small impish woman perfectly described by her name. 'I've seen lots of people getting your name. I'm so thrilled with the window you made. I hope it brings you lots of business.'

'Even if nothing comes from it, thanks a lot for giving me this opportunity. It will be a big help in getting started.'

Merry stuck her arm through Erin's. 'I'm sorry you had to come home to take care of your mom, but it sure has been my gain. How is she, anyway?'

'Doing very well. She has only a slight hesitation in her speech, and barely limps. The family is delighted that she's back in the kitchen. Nicky said if he had to eat much more of my cooking, he was moving out.'

'What a nice family you have. I'm so glad that your mom is better.'

'We were lucky,' Erin said soberly. 'The doctor said that the stroke was very minor. Hopefully, with care, any more can be averted. Incidentally, Mom told me to ask you to come and visit her soon.'

'I'd love to.' Merry looked around. 'But, right now I'd better get back to my hostess duties. I see that people are starting to wander towards the door.'

'I'd better do the same. Thanks again.'

Merry frowned. 'If I'd known you were coming alone I'd have suggested you spend the night. Why don't you do that anyway? I'll lend you a nightie. I don't like the idea of your driving all the way back to Denver this late at night.'

'Neither do I.'

Erin turned in surprise. She hadn't seen Tony approaching. 'It's not like you live in Outer Mongolia, you know. Parker to home is only about a forty-five-minute drive. I'll lock my doors,' she assured Merry.

'Even if it's a five-minute drive, that's too far this late at night,' Tony said.

'You're as bad as my brothers. I'll be all right.'

'I can drop you off when I take Jennifer home.'

'Be serious. I'm a big girl now. Twenty-three years old. I can handle myself.' Before Tony could argue any more, Erin headed for the door. Because so many people stopped her to chat, getting to her car took longer than she expected. At least Tony Hart didn't harass her any more about going with him. She had to admit that his retreat surprised her. He didn't appear to be a man who gave up so easily.

Minutes later, driving along Parker Road, Erin was wishing she had paid more attention to Tony and Merry. Or less. If they hadn't brought the subject up, she wouldn't be so nervous now. No doubt it was entirely her imagination that a car was following her. Lots of people from the party were probably going in the same direction as she was. The trouble was, whenever she slowed down so that the following car could pass, the other driver slowed down, too. Sitting at a red light, Erin checked for the umpteenth time that her doors were all securely locked.

The light turned green and she sped away. The yellow lights in her rear-view mirror stayed with her. 'Calm down, Erin,' she told herself. The light ahead turned red, and Erin eased to a stop. Nervously she checked the mirror again. Still there. Another car pulled up in the lane beside her. Rock music blared from open windows. Maybe here was help. Erin glanced over. Loud catcalls and whistles greeted her. Great. A carload of college kids, obviously drunk. The occupants of the car tumbled out and surrounded Erin's car, hollering and pounding on her bonnet. Immediately she recalled the incident she had read about in the paper where a bunch of college kids out in California had pulled two girls out of their car and ripped off their clothes. That was a convertible, she reminded herself, pretending to ignore the obnoxious behaviour outside her car, and at the same time trying very hard to hold back tears.

Suddenly a deep voice cut through the raucous clamour, and Erin looked on in astonishment as her tormentors backed away, sheepish expressions on their faces. Tumbling into their car, they sped away. A tapping on her window claimed Erin's attention.

A familiar face peered in at her. 'You OK?'

Shakily Erin rolled down her window. 'Yes. Thank you. I appreciate your stopping. They had me a little nervous.'

'Dumb kids,' Tony muttered. 'Too much money and too much time. They think it's adult to drink, at the same time ignoring the responsibilities that go along with alcohol consumption. I doubt they'll bother you any more, but just in case, we'll follow you the rest of the way home.'

'Well, thanks again.' So much for her vaunted independence. She didn't even suggest that his following her wasn't necessary. A little giggle bubbled up in her throat. What must Jennifer think about Tony's escorting another woman home? Erin had caught a shadowy glimpse of the other woman sitting in Tony's car after he had chased the boys off.

Tony stayed behind Erin all the way to her house. As she walked to the front door, he tooted his car horn and drove away. Erin had to admit, when it came to playing games, Tony knew all the moves. On the other hand, whatever Tony's motives for following her this evening, she couldn't deny that his actions had rescued her from an uncomfortable, if not dangerous, situation. She thought of the grin on Tony's face when she had weakly accepted his assurance that he would follow her the rest of the way home. The idea of being grateful to him didn't sit well with her. She knew his type. He was challenged by her indifference to him. Knowing that she was now obliged to him would amuse him. She wondered how long it would be before Tony followed up on his advantage.

Not long. When the doorbell rang Sunday noon, Erin went to answer the door, totally unsuspecting. 'You!'

Tony grinned down at her. 'Made it home OK last night, did you?' The twinkle in his eyes confirmed her suspicions. He was definitely amused.

'Who's that at the door?' Erin's father appeared in the front hall.

Tony stepped forward, stretching out his hand. 'Tony Hart, Mr Cassidy.'

'Doyle Cassidy,' Erin's father said eagerly. 'Nice to meet you. Think you'll get to the Super Bowl this year?'

'Plan to.'

Erin listened in exasperation as the two men quickly became absorbed in football talk. Surely Tony hadn't driven all the way out here to discuss the Explorers' play-off chances. She edged past them into the living-room.

Martin stood up. 'Ready?' At her assurance that she was, he made polite farewells to Erin's mother, and they turned to leave.

Tony followed Doyle into the room, stopping abruptly at the sight of Erin slinging a bag over her shoulder. 'Going somewhere?'

'Martin and I are going to lunch and a special art exhibit down in Larimer Square.' She turned to the man behind her. 'Martin, this is Tony Hart. Tony, Martin Thomas.'

The two men shook hands. It wasn't Martin's fault that his slight build made him look puny and under-nourished beside Tony, Erin assured herself. She ignored the mocking look of interrogation that Tony sent her way. Martin possessed brain, not brawn.

'I came over to discuss my window,' Tony said plaintively.

'You should have called and made an appointment,' Erin said briskly.

'Can we make one now?' he asked humbly.

Erin eyed him suspiciously. Now what? 'Tomorrow is fine for me.'

Agreeing to that, they made arrangements to meet in the morning at the studio. Tony made motions to leave, but Doyle grabbed his arm. 'Stay to lunch,' he urged. 'We're eating in about an hour, aren't we, Carrie?'

Erin's mother joined her husband in urging that Tony stay. Not that it took much urging, Erin noted cynically. The delectable smells of a pot roast wafted down the hall and into the living-room as she and Martin left.

'What'd he want?' Martin asked as Erin fastened her seat-belt.

'What he said. He's asked me to design a window for him.'

'Likely story.'

'You don't believe me?' Erin asked in surprise.

Martin reached over and patted her hand. 'Sure, I believe you. It's him I'm not so sure about. I've heard about his reputation. A man like him isn't going to let a beauty like you escape his clutches.'

Aware that she had had much the same suspicion, Erin couldn't argue with his conclusions. The afternoon passed in a blur for her, the pleasure in the long-anticipated exhibition ruined by her thoughts constantly returning to what was happening in her own home. What in the world were Tony and her family talking about? Would they see through the alleged purpose of his visit, and understand, as Martin did, that it wasn't her work that Tony was interested in? She didn't fool herself for one minute that Tony found her irresistible. On the contrary, it was Tony who thought that he was irresistible, and the discovery that Erin didn't find him so galled him, and spurred him on to make the conquest.

He might think that winning over her family would be the first step in his campaign to win her over. Little did he realise how that would work against him. Her family already suffered from

football fever. If Tony ate with his fingers and
wiped his mouth on his shirt sleeve, her father and
brother would overlook it because of his football
statistics. At least she didn't have to sit there and
endure their boring conversation. She wondered
how Tony would manage to bring her name into
the conversation. Surely he would try to gather
some information about her that he could use in
his pursuit.

'Of course we didn't spend all our time talking
about you,' her mother reproved her later that
evening. 'I'm not sure your name even came up.
Between Nicky and your father, the whole dinner-
table conversation was football, football and more
football.'

'You poor thing,' Erin immediately sym-
pathised. 'I know how sports bore you.'

'Maybe I've been a little hasty in my judge-
ments,' Carolyn said, to Erin's complete surprise.
'I never before thought about the intellectual aspects, the planning and strategy that go into a game
plan. Tony is certainly no dumb athlete. Did you
know that he was a Rhodes scholar?'

'He just told you that to get on your good side,'
Erin derided.

'No,' Carolyn said firmly. 'He didn't mention it
at all. Nicky told me after Tony had left.'

'You better be careful, Mom,' Erin teased.
'You'll be written up in the paper as Tony's latest
heart-throb.'

Carolyn giggled like a young girl. 'He did say if
I hadn't already been married, he'd propose on the
spot. Sometimes a good apple pie gets you further
than a pretty face.'

A good apple pie, indeed, Erin thought in fond
exasperation the next day as she pottered around

her workshop waiting for Tony. You'd think being the personal cook and maid for six males would have pushed her mother into rebellion by now. Not so. Carolyn felt there was no higher calling than keeping her men happy. Not a conviction shared by Erin. There had been a good bit of grumbling among the Cassidy men when Carolyn had her stroke and Erin had come back from Phoenix and taken over the household management, assigning chores to everyone. He who eats, works, was her very unpopular motto. All had sighed with relief when Carolyn had recovered enough to insist on 'doing her duty.' Now only Erin helped her mother out. And, she thought, guiltily, not as much as she should. When it came to a choice between doing the laundry and working in her studio, the studio came first every time. Maybe there were people in this world who enjoyed cleaning toilets, but she wasn't one of them. No wonder men hated the idea of liberation and equality for women. Who wouldn't hate to give up the idea of free maid-service? She looked around the cluttered work-room. She could use a little maid-service herself.

Grabbing a broom, she began to sweep the floor. With Tony due any minute now, this wasn't the time to work on any of her glass projects. No one knew better than she how absorbed she could become. And how dirty. She had debated at great length what to wear, a circumstance that irritated her as soon as she had realised what she was doing. Tony Hart was no different from any other client. It was her glass work that he was coming to see, not her. If only her heart and breathing could be convinced of that and slow down a little. Of course it was natural that she was nervous. A successful commission for Tony Hart could be a tremendous boost to her fledgling business. Erin would be the first to admit that she was by no means self-supporting, but each commission had led to another, and she had been optimistic about her future when Mrs Filmore had come her way. She sighed. Mrs Filmore was in the past. That was why she was forced to accept Tony Hart's commission.

Footsteps could be heard on the outside staircase taking every other step in stride. Tony's ruggedly handsome face appeared in the open doorway. 'So this is where you create.'

'Come into my parlour...'

Tony grinned. 'Is that a warning?'

'Warning?'

'That if I don't watch out, I'll fall into your trap.'

'What trap is that?' Erin asked.

'The one all you single women set for us unsuspecting bachelors.'

'Your marital status is absolutely of no interest to me,' Erin said coldly.

Tony turned up his shirt collar and shivered ostentatiously. 'Brrr. The lady is afraid to flirt.'

'I'm not afraid. I just don't think that sexual repartee has any part in the business world. And in this particular case, you're here only as a potential customer,' she reminded him.

'In other words, if I want to tell you how beautiful you look this morning, I have to wait until after office hours.'

'Exactly,' Erin snapped a moment too soon. Her face reddened as she realised that she'd fallen into a trap. Agreeing with him was the same as accepting his compliment.

A wicked look gleamed in Tony's eyes as he recognised her confusion. 'I like what you're wearing, too. Jeans must have been invented for women with, er, figures like yours.' A slow, deliberate study left Erin in no doubt as to what he meant by 'figure'.

Her face flushed, she thrust some folders at Tony. 'Here are photos of windows I've done for clients, as well as a number of magazine clippings of windows. I draw original cartoons for all the windows that I do, but if you'll look through these and point out which ones appeal to you, that will tell me what style you like.'

Tony laid the folders down. 'I have a better idea. Come out and see my house and where I want the window. That should tell you everything you need to know about my taste, and then you can decide what would be suitable.'

Two emotions warred within Erin. She wasn't sure she trusted him enough to go out to his house with him, but on the other hand, she would have to go there some time. Surely she was capable of dealing with any passes he would try to throw her way.

Securing her thick mane of hair at the back of her neck with a colourful scarf, she sat in the front seat of Tony's sports car and gazed out of the window. April was continuing to bless the Denver area with warmth and sunshine, and over in the park, joggers and cyclists were taking advantage of the beautiful weather. Canada geese sailed smoothly along the shoreline of Sloan Lake, ignoring the activity on the path. A yellow butterfly floated from one blossom-laden stalk of indigo-blue grape hyacinths to another. Erin envied their serenity. The small sports car seemed confining, and she was uneasily aware of the large, capable hand which rested on the gear lever only inches from her left knee.

'You didn't ask, but since you're no doubt dying to know, let me assure you that the body shop was able to cover the scratches in the bonnet, and this baby looks as good as new.' There was unquestionably an undercurrent of sarcasm in Tony's voice.

Erin looked down her nose. 'How nice for you.'

'You're a real tough nut, aren't you?' he asked drily.

'If I wasn't a tough nut, as you call me, I wouldn't have lasted long. Not with five brothers.' She had spent all her life surrounded by males, her brothers and their innumerable friends, which made it all the crazier that this one man had the power to disconcert her. Tony shifted, drawing her attention to the ripple of muscles in his right forearm. The air inside the car was suddenly stifling and Erin fought an overwhelming sense of claustrophobia. 'Tell me about your family,' she said desperately.

'You've met Allie, and I have one younger brother. He teaches in Boulder.' From that point on Tony took control of the conversation with a polished ease that Erin couldn't help but envy. Of course, she reminded herself firmly, one didn't gain a reputation for being a ladies' man by being an inarticulate clod. If there was one thing that Tony Hart had, it was an abundance of experience. Pursuing women was just a game to him, a game for which he had written all the rules.

Unwillingly she laughed at an outrageous story Tony told of his youth. In spite of her inner misgivings, she found herself being disarmed by his easy flow of amusing family anecdotes. His strict avoidance of flirtatious remarks made her begin to wonder if she had misjudged him. No doubt in his position he was so accustomed to women falling all over him that he hadn't realised at the beginning that Erin wasn't interested in him. Now that he knew it, he was accepting it and treating her as just another business acquaintance. She relaxed against the back of the seat.

The miles clicked pleasantly away and Erin looked up in surprise as they pulled into the housing area where Merry lived. 'I didn't realise your house was here.'

'Merry sold me on the area,' he said as he pulled into the driveway of a modern cedar-clad house that backed on to the golf course only a couple of blocks up from the Robertses.

'Very nice,' Erin approved before following Tony into a large room littered with sawdust and wood chips. An enormous electric saw and bench sat idle in one corner. 'Where are all the workers?'

'Right here.'

'You?'

One blond eyebrow lifted at the scepticism in her voice. 'Why so surprised? I've always liked to work with my hands, so I decided to spend the off-season finishing the inside of my house. I've had some help with the plumbing and the electricity. I'm not that excited about doing it. But the wood,' he caressed a beautifully-fitted doorjamb, 'that's different. Come on. I'll show you around.'

Erin followed him in mounting disbelief. While many of the rooms were still raw shells, others held examples of some of the finest woodcraft that Erin had ever seen. Exquisite wood detailing, a beautifully carved fireplace and unusual built-in cupboards all captivated the eye. Erin's obvious pleasure in Tony's work and her honest enthusiasm soon melted the barriers of constraint between them. In one of the rooms a rocking-chair provided a touch of whimsy with a carved cat sleeping on one of the rockers.

Erin looked at Tony. 'Yours?'

'My mom had a cat who used to like to sleep on her rocker like that, and Mom would forget and start to rock, dislodging him. It gave me the idea. I made it several years ago.' He absent-mindedly rubbed the back of the chair.

No wonder all the pieces had such a deep sheen, Erin thought. Tony seemed to be unable to pass by any of his work without touching it, unconsciously displaying his love for the wood. This unexpected facet of Tony's personality stunned Erin. She found it difficult to reconcile his beautiful and sensitive craftsmanship with the image of a sweaty football player whose only goals were to score on the field and in the bedroom.

Eventually Erin found herself in the kitchen, aware that Tony's house had given her a new and surprising perspective of him. No one who did such beautiful work with his hands could possibly be as shallow and conceited as Nicky's magazine had painted Tony. She smiled warmly at him as he handed her a glass of iced tea. 'I love this house.'

'Want to move in?' he asked lightly.

'Well, not today. I have to do my laundry,' she said, treating the question as frivolously as he had meant it.

Tony winced. 'You really know how to hurt a guy. Rejected for a pile of dirty clothes.'

Leaning back against the counter, Erin shrugged. 'Rejection is good for you.'

Tony put down his glass. 'No, it's not.' He moved closer to Erin, and placed his hands on either side of the counter behind her, his chest lightly pressing against hers.

He's going to kiss me, Erin thought, and she wondered why she didn't mind.

'Since you could say we're on a coffee-break right now, is it safe for me to tell you how beautiful you are?'

Fascinated by the way Tony's eyes darkened as he stared down into her upturned face, Erin remained silent. Seeing his house made her aware that he was a man with a deep appreciation of beauty, and she was inordinately pleased by his compliment.

Interpreting her silence as an invitation to continue, Tony bent his head to hers. Erin's eyes flickered closed, shutting out the intense look on Tony's face. His lips were feather-soft upon hers and she responded shyly. His work had created a bond between them, a bond composed of a shared appreciation of all that was beautiful. Tony deepened the kiss, encouraging Erin's lips to part, allowing him access. She shuddered with feeling as he probed the moist inner reaches of her mouth. His large hands untied the scarf that confined her hair, and a black mane tumbled to her shoulders. He combed the heavy mass with his fingers, his touch light and sensuous upon her scalp. The faint scent of aftershave teased at Erin's nostrils while the smells of fresh wood and varnish were strong in the room. Erin wondered if she would ever be able to smell them again without remembering this moment.

Through the open screen door drifted the voices of players on the golf course and the distinctive calls of a meadowlark. Tony's lips left hers, and traced a path across her cheek bone. He lifted her hair from her neck and feathered a row of kisses under her ear and down towards her open collar. The pulse at the base of her throat beat harder, catching his attention. Her head thrown back, Erin kneaded the muscles in his wide shoulders. When his mouth finally returned to hers, she joyfully welcomed the feel and taste of him. Her fingers twined through his coarse, blond hair, revelling in its springy texture.

Tony pressed gentle kisses along the rim of her mouth. 'We'd better go up to the bedroom,' he muttered.

His words were a dash of cold water, and she pulled back from his embrace. 'Sex! Is that all you ever think about?'

He studied her with heavy-lidded eyes. 'You didn't seem to be objecting a minute ago. Unless I imagined your, er, enthusiastic response.'

Erin was too angry and humiliated to speak. Her cheeks flushed with fury, she struggled to fasten her scarf back around her hair with fingers that trembled and failed to do her will. Tony brushed her hands aside and finished the task. No doubt he had plenty of experience, Erin thought bitterly. How could she have let her enthusiasm about Tony's unexpected artistic talents make her forget that he had the personality and morals of a tomcat? With her own eyes she had seen him at the party pursuing one woman while the escort of another. He was undoubtedly one of those men who were so insecure that they measured their masculinity by the number of women they bedded a week. Well, she wasn't about to help him meet this week's quota.

'Made up your mind?'

'What?' She stared stupidly at him.

'I can see those thoughts racing around your little head. Do I want to work for this sex fiend? What will I have to put up with while I make his window?'

The window. Erin had completely forgotten why she was here in his house in the first place. Her blank face gave her away.

Tony laughed unpleasantly. 'Don't tell me that one kiss so distracted Little Miss Prude that she can't remember why she is here.'

Erin struggled for composure. 'No such thing. You flatter yourself if you think that a kiss from you can cause me to lose control.' She felt herself blushing at his sarcastic look. 'You've had it in mind to seduce me since Merry's party. Now that you know I'm not interested, I see no reason why we can't maintain our relationship on a purely business level. I'm willing to forget that this unfortunate incident ever took place.'

'A beautiful speech,' he applauded softly. 'What if I'm not willing to forget this unfortunate incident?' He mocked her words. 'You won't mind if, while we're discussing contracts and bills, I'm remembering the taste of your mouth and the silky feel of your hair, will you?'

The stiffening fled from Erin's knees at the image that his words evoked. She wouldn't, couldn't, work with this man. She opened her mouth to say so.

'Never mind. That haughty, sour-puss expression on your face would chill the most fervent lover. Already I'm beginning to believe that your response was merely a figment of my imagination. No doubt by tomorrow I'll have forgotten we ever kissed.'

'With a sex life as active as yours, I can well believe that,' Erin flashed. 'I'm sure our kiss meant nothing to you.'

'Are you saying it meant something to you?' Tony asked sceptically.

About to deny that a kiss from him could possibly have any significance to her, Erin saw the wooden cat peering through an open doorway at her from his permanent perch on the rocker. Taking a deep breath, she forced herself to answer honestly, even if Tony laughed at her. 'When you've won a difficult game, aren't you so exhilarated by your victory that you need to share your feelings?'

Tony looked at her in astonishment. 'I suppose so,' he said slowly.

'I feel the same way when I see something beautiful. Like your work here. You have such a talent for creating beauty that I was stunned by it. The kiss was as if the artist in me were saluting the artist in you.' She added bitterly, 'For a moment I forgot that sex was just another game to you. Another athletic arena in which you obviously excel.'

Tony started to say something, evidently thought better of it, and turned away, heading towards the kitchen door. 'Let me show you where I thought the window should go.'

Good. That meant the subject of the kiss was closed. Tony led her upstairs to a large room. French doors at the far end led to a deck and a panoramic view of the Rockies in the distance. But that wasn't what caused Erin to panic on the threshold of the room. Against one wall was an enormous four-poster bed with pencil posts rising to the ceiling. A pale cream coverlet was spread over the mattress. Surely Tony wouldn't... Her mind refused to carry the thought any further.

Realising that she was still in the hall, Tony swung around on his heels. The quizzical expression on his face was immediately replaced by one filled with mockery. 'Your opinion of my morals is hardly flattering. There are enough willing women around, I don't need to resort to force.' He paused. 'Your mind made the leap from one kiss to my bed with flattering speed. Which poses the interesting question: would I need force?'

'Yes,' Erin snapped.

Tony shrugged. 'I wouldn't have thought so, but you ought to know your own self best.'

'You're cheap and disgusting,' Erin cried. 'Making fun of other people's emotions. You're nothing but...but an animal.' She turned to leave.

'If you're through venting your spleen,' Tony's voice was bored, 'do you suppose we could get on with business?'

Erin paused at the top of the staircase. As much as she longed to tell Tony she would rather die than make him a window, the fact remained, if she wanted to make a success of her business, she could hardly afford to turn down his commission. Reluctantly she returned to the bedroom.

Tony greeted her return with a derisive look, but made no comment. Taking hold of her arm, he pulled her further into the room and pointed to a large round window placed high in the wall on the east side of the room where the morning sun would shine in on the bed. 'I want that window filled in with stained glass. Can you do it?'

'Yes.' She ignored the burning patch on her arm where his hand still rested. 'I'll need the dimensions. What kind of design do you have in mind?'

'I thought I'd leave that to you. You're the artist. You've seen my house. Surprise me.'

CHAPTER THREE

SURPRISE him, Tony had said. Well, he was certainly going to be surprised. Erin thrust aside the small pangs of conscience that nagged at her as she studied the window cartoon before her. Hadn't Tony said he liked naked women?

Erin rolled up the pattern and set it aside. No telling when Tony would come in to see it. He hadn't been home when she had called, so she had left a message on his answering machine. Meanwhile, she had other work awaiting her attention.

Concentrating on the task in front of her, Erin didn't hear Tony's arrival.

'I'd hate to meet you in a dark alley if you were carrying that,' Tony's voice said from the open doorway.

'This?' Erin held up the wickedly curved knife. 'It's for cutting the lead. See?' She rocked the knife easily across the lead, producing a sharp cut.

Tony walked over to the workbench and watched her. Moulding the cut lead around a piece of glass, Erin deftly fitted it into the half-completed window, hammering a horseshoe nail firmly against it to hold the glass in place. Putting down her tools, she wiped her hands on her already dirty jeans, and walked over to the other workbench and pointed to a brown roll of paper. 'Here's your window.'

Tony unrolled the paper, and leaned over the table, his large hands holding the edges of the paper to keep it from rerolling. He studied the design, a muscle beside his mouth starting to clench. Erin carefully surveyed her stained fingers.

'I suppose this is your idea of a joke,' he finally said in a tight voice. He swept the pattern off the table. 'Where's the real design?'

Erin concentrated on watching the cartoon hit the floor and roll loosely up. 'That is the real design. Don't you like it? I thought it would appeal to your more prurient interests. I thought you would be pleased.'

'The hell you did.'

'I did,' Erin protested. 'I tried to come up with a design that you and your friends could enjoy. I didn't want something too sophisticated. You were the one who said you wanted naked women,' she added defensively.

'You were well aware that I was joking. And if you're trying to convince me that you came up with this design just because you think I'm a dumb jock, unable to appreciate fine art, save your breath. We both know what this is all about. You're still angry about that kiss.'

'That's not true,' Erin said coldly. 'I told you I needed more information about what kind of design you wanted. If you had something specific in mind, you should have said so.'

'What you mean is, I shouldn't have trusted you. I should have realised that you can't forgive the fact that you responded to an "animal" like me,' he charged with brutal sarcasm.

'I didn't respond to you at all.' At the incredulous look on his face, she hastily added, 'I responded, if to anything, to the person I thought you were, a person of taste and refinement, a person who doesn't even exist.'

'That Martin follow looks like a person of taste and refinement. Do you melt in his arms, too?'

'What a crude remark,' Erin snapped.

'That's an athlete for you. Crude and disgusting. Panting after every woman like a stag in rut. Too bad for you that muscles are what turns you on. Admit it.'

'No such thing!'

'Take those ridiculous goggles off.'

'I will not!' Erin had even forgotten she still had her safety goggles on.

Tony jerked them off her head, freeing her hair from the headscarf that covered it at the same time. 'There. That's better,' he said with satisfaction.

'What...what are you...doing?' she stammered, her pulse racing at the determined gleam in his darkened blue eyes.

'Try not to be stupid,' he murmured sardonically as his head dipped towards hers.

Common sense warned her not to fight him. Her workshop was too small, too cluttered with dangerous tools and jutting pieces of glass to serve as a safe arena. Best to endure his embrace, making it clear to him that she derived no pleasure from his arms. She stilled a responsive quiver as he brushed his hand softly across her cheek.

'No wonder you need those goggles,' he said. 'You have tiny chunks of glass stuck all over your face.'

His mouth pressed to hers prevented any answer she might have made. By then her only concern was fighting her body's tendency to melt into his arms. By dint of tremendous effort, she remained passive, her mouth refusing to soften, her arms leaden pipes at her side. Resisting all efforts by Tony to get her to part her lips, she reminded herself over and over again that Tony's sole reason for this sadistic treatment was to get her to admit that she desired him. She didn't. She couldn't. Not a man who saw women, not as individuals, but as sex objects, put on earth solely to entertain and worship him.

Tony stepped back, his eyes glinting darkly at her. 'You win. This time. I'll be back the day after tomorrow and this time I expect to see a design worthy of my house. And of you. You put another piece of trash like this in front of me, and I'm likely to toss you over my knee and paddle the daylights out of you.'

'How dare you! Is that how you do business with men?' Erin cried. 'Do you threaten to spank them when you're not happy with their work? Or is that a technique that you save especially for the ladies?'

'Some men have tried to cheat me and others have done sloppy work. But none have tried to deliberately provoke me, and you know damn well that's what you've done here. Strictly business, you keep saying. That design wasn't business and you know it. I got under your skin the other day, and you're trying to hit back at me. Well, forget it, lady, because I don't care what your opinion of me is. All I want out of you is a first-class window, and I damn well better get it. Understood?'

'If you're not happy with my work, you're welcome to go elsewhere,' Erin said stiffly.

'You'd like that, wouldn't you?' He grabbed her around the back of her neck, pulling her tight against his body. 'You started the game at Merry's party. Flipping that sensuous body around in the football game, pretending to be somebody else. What's the matter? Now that I've taken up your challenge, are you afraid that the game is over your head'? Too bad, because it's not over until the final gun goes off.' He pressed a firm kiss against her unyielding lips. 'Day after tomorrow.'

Shaken by Tony's words, Erin leaned against the work bench, listening to the sound of his footsteps running lightly down the outside staircase. He was obviously undisturbed by their heated argument, not moved by the meeting of their lips. Darn him. He was even whistling. An unwilling grin twisted her lips as the unmistakable melody of 'When Irish Eyes Are Smiling' wafted up through the open doorway.

The smile faded away as she looked down at the brown paper curled up at her feet. Tony was right. If she couldn't separate her personal feelings from her business, what right did she have to berate him for the same thing? Erin kicked aside the cartoon. Pride in her work should have prevented the incident which had just occurred. If she had been professional in her dealings with Tony, then he wouldn't have felt justified in reacting to her design in a purely personal manner.

There was no denying that the window was designed with malicious intent. She had been offended by Tony's kiss the other day. No, that wasn't true. It wasn't the kiss that upset her, it was Tony's reception of it. The discovery of his artistic genius had momentarily inflamed her senses, aroused her passions. But what for her was a beautiful moment had been ruined by Tony's earthy desires. He had used his art to play on her emotions much as he used his fame from the football field to entice other women into his bed. All she meant to him was another notch in his belt, and that realisation hurt and humiliated her. The design was her way of striking back. She had only been lying to herself in

trying to believe that he would like it and approve
it. Her emotions had overruled her head. An indul-
gence she could ill afford. It would have served her
right if Tony had taken his business elsewhere.

Erin leaned down and picked up the cartoon,
tossing it into a nearby wastebasket. She was a
professional, and this time, she would turn out a
product that she could be proud of. A horrid
thought suddenly struck her. What if Tony had
liked the design? She started to giggle helplessly.
Fortunately Tony had not hit upon the ultimate revenge—making her build that perfectly awful
window.

The new design met with Tony's approval.
Thinking back to the neutral colour-scheme of
Tony's bedroom, Erin had been struck by the
soothing mixture of blond woods and textured white
fabrics. The swirling lines and curves reminiscent
of art nouveau and the jewel colours of her design
were meant to provide startling contrast to the
spartan simplicity of the bedroom. Women with
Beardsley-like profiles and billowing hair were
tucked among exotic flowering vines, evoking
images of richness and opulence. The design was
alive with birds and butterflies, as well as the sty-
lised leaves and overblown flowers. Influenced by
a picture of some William Morris wallpapers, she
had selected rich blues and browns, with rose ac-
cents. Secretly worried that Tony would reject the
design as too ornate, she was pleased that he listened carefully to her reasoning and then approved
the design without hesitation. Agreeing with her
colour-scheme, he had left the selection of the glass
to her. No comment had been made about the pre-
vious design. They had both maintained a cool,
businesslike attitude throughout the entire encounter. There had been no accidental brushing up

against her body, no intimate, teasing looks, no stolen kisses. Just exactly how Erin wanted it. Which didn't explain why she felt so unsettled long after Tony had gone.

Maybe because he hadn't gone far. Just out into the park to toss a football around with Nicky. Their laughing voices had come floating up through the open windows of the studio. Finally she had turned on her grinder to drown out the unwelcome sounds. Unfortunately, for some reason, she still hadn't been able to concentrate on her work, and as a result had ground too much off several pieces of glass, forcing her to recut them. It didn't help that she nicked her fingers several times in the process.

She detested the way that Tony Hart got under her skin. He wasn't right. She couldn't like him. OK, so maybe her body did betray her when he was around. But what he called desire could be nothing more than her artistic self admiring the perfection of the male form. That must be it. Artists through the years had been intrigued with the unclothed human body. It was one thing to admire it, it was another to become obsessed with it. If she didn't stop thinking about Tony, she was in danger of that very thing.

Painting, admiring, sculpting the human form said nothing about the human mind. A perfectly beautiful woman could have the brain of a pea. She and Tony had nothing in common except a shared interest in creating beautiful things. She admitted that he was devastatingly handsome in a rugged sort of way. She admired his body. And his kisses had been . . . pleasant. But that was all. There was no way that she could be interested in him as a person. He was an athlete. A man who made his living throwing a silly little ball.

Perhaps she might have unwittingly succumbed to his obvious charms if it hadn't been for her first two encounters with him. Erin's brothers insisted that she held a grudge longer than anyone they knew, but she couldn't help it that when she thought of Tony she thought first of his lack of contrition over the accident and his lack of compassion over what to her was such a serious setback. In retrospect she realised that his initial anger had been based on concern for his sister, and that he had been rushing to Allie's defence. This didn't excuse the fact that he had never apologised to Erin for what had happened. Apparently he felt the great Tony Hart was above admitting fault. And then there was his rude and egotistical behaviour at Merry's party: abandoning his date while he chased after Erin. He was like a child who always wanted the toy that he didn't have.

All of which wouldn't have mattered so much if it weren't for the fact that the Cassidy family had warmly welcomed Tony into their midst, a circumstance which irritated Erin, but failed to surprise her. She had realised for years that the male members of her family lived, breathed and dreamed football. Tony had even managed to ingratiate himself into her mother's graces so that she was constantly inviting him to dinner. Of course, the man oozed dangerous amounts of charm and charisma. Carolyn Cassidy insisted that Tony liked the way they treated him as if he were one of the family, a viewpoint that Erin took exception to. Couldn't her mother see that Tony lapped up the adulation of Doyle and her brothers? He enjoyed the way they hung on his every word. Erin pretended that her family's attitude didn't bother her, but their hero-worship nauseated her. All Tony ever talked about was first downs, and yards gained, and other non-sense like that. He never concerned himself with real life. What were his opinions on nuclear energy? What did he think about the children starving in Africa? And if he had any opinion on the forth-coming elections, Erin had certainly never heard it. When did you ever ask him, a tiny little voice probed.

One result of Tony's invasion of her home was that Erin found herself spending more time with Martin. Where before she had been content to let him set the pace of their friendship, she now found herself calling him on the phone and arranging to meet him. What Martin thought of her more ag-gressive behaviour, she didn't know.

Tony, however, did not bother to keep his thoughts to himself. 'Running away with Martin again tonight?' he asked as he ambled into the house in Nicky's wake and found her standing in the hall, obviously dressed to go out. 'What is it this time? The ballet? A poetry reading?'

Erin was aware that an instant antagonism had flared up between the two men. She suspected that Martin felt threatened by the brawn and rampant masculinity of Tony. Tony was obviously uncom-fortable with Martin's sophisticated tastes, and lost no opportunity to mock him and his interests. Her voice was cool as she acknowledged his latest taunt. 'I'm not running away. And we are going out to dinner.'

'To a quaint little bistro, no doubt, where Martin will peruse the wine list and impress you with his knowledge and good taste.'

'It may come as some surprise to you, but Martin is a gentleman,' Erin said haughtily.

'You're right. It would surprise me. One of those, is he?'

'No, he is not,' Erin gritted between her teeth. 'Whatever one of those is,' she added belatedly.

Tony just laughed and disappeared up the staircase with an insolent wave, leaving Erin seething with annoyance at the bottom of the steps.

Her mood was not improved when Martin, seeing Tony's car in the driveway, began denigrating every person who ever participated in sports, forcing Erin, out of loyalty, to defend her brothers, a defence which Martin chose to believe included Tony. That, in turn, necessitated her spending the rest of the evening trying to coax Martin out of a petulant mood. She was relieved when the evening finally ended. Martin apologised on the doorstep for being such unpleasant company, and Erin readily forgave him. It was understandable that Tony's macho personality could seem threatening to someone like Martin. She simply had to convince him that men like Tony didn't appeal to her.

Tony's constant presence certainly didn't help reassure Martin. And it didn't help that the next time Martin came to pick her up, Erin was involved in a heavy discussion with Tony and her family as to whether the lessons learned on playing fields could be directly related to life. The fact that she and Tony were on opposite sides of the argument was lost on Martin.

'I've never played any sport in my life, and I don't think that my life is blighted because of it,' Erin pointed out.

'Come on, Erin. You're a girl. Girls don't count,' Nicky protested.

Tony grinned wryly at Erin. 'Does this kid have a lot to learn.'

'You know what I mean, Tony,' Nicky said, blushing hotly. 'Playing games teaches a man how to think.'

'Women don't need to think?' Erin challenged.

'It's not a question of whether you need to, Erin. Face it. No one in this family will ever accuse you of doing it,' Nicky said.

Erin pummelled her younger brother with a sofa pillow until he yelled for mercy, seeing that Tony and his father had no intention of coming to his rescue.

'You've got more guts than me,' Tony said, laughing at the teenager. 'One thing I've learned over the years is that liberated women take a back seat to no man. On the other hand, you're right about sports teaching players to think. For example, a lot of people believe all you need to play quarterback is a strong arm, but that's only part of it. I do a lot of homework before I ever go on the field. I watch tapes of the other teams, see where their strengths and weaknesses are. Out on the field I have a constant stream of data running through my head—does one of their defenders look tired, giving us an edge, or is one of my receivers being too loosely covered? I have only seconds to make a decision, and the consequences of that decision fall on me. Sure, I'll get the credit for a touchdown pass, but I'll also get booed if I get intercepted. Isn't that what life is all about? Considering all your options, picking the best, and living with the consequences?'

'The difference is, if you pick the wrong option, it doesn't really matter,' Martin said in chilly disdain from the doorway. 'Football isn't exactly a life-or-death situation.'

'Neither is deciding what deodorant to wear, but you advertising guys sure try to convince people that it is.' Nicky instantly defended his hero.

'Calm down, fella. Martin is entitled to his opinions.' Cool laughter lurked in the depths of Tony's blue eyes as he turned to Martin. 'Considering the time Nicky spends in locker-rooms, you'd think he'd realise the importance of a good deodorant.'

'I don't handle deodorants,' Martin said stiffly.

'Martin! I didn't hear the doorbell.' Erin rushed to intercede. 'I'm ready.' She hustled him out of the door, but she was too late to prevent wounded feelings.

'He's just showing off for your benefit,' Martin grumbled, his feelings exacerbated by what he perceived as Tony's mockery.

'If he is, he's wasting his time,' Erin said briskly. 'I'm totally in agreement with you.'

Martin was not convinced, and Erin spent most of the evening soothing his ruffled feathers. Another black mark to chalk up against Tony Hart. She had been doing just fine until he came along. He had caused problems with her business, he had practically moved into her home, and now he was baiting her boyfriend. She was getting sick and tired of his disruptive influence in her life.

A few days later Erin was still cataloguing Tony's sins as she drove home from an appointment with a new client. For over twenty-three years she had managed just beautifully without ever hearing the name Tony Hart. Now, not a day went by that someone wasn't drumming the fact of his existence into her head. If it wasn't Martin complaining about him, or Nicky and her father quoting him, it was her mother worrying about his diet. And when she retreated to her workshop, the work in progress was his window. She couldn't seem to escape the man. And what was worse, she suspected that Tony was well aware of her irritation and highly amused by it.

A gust of wind shook the car, tearing her thoughts from Tony, as she glanced uneasily at the blackened sky overhead. The radio had issued winter storm warnings for the foothills and eastern plains today, but since the weatherman's forecasts had been off a hundred and eighty degrees lately, Erin had been confident that the day would remain clear and sunny and had driven blithely off to Elizabeth, a small town on the plains southeast of Denver. Apparently, for once the weatherman was going to be right on the mark. The fact that it was April made no difference, because Colorado weather was totally unpredictable and certainly disrespectful of any calendar. Spring blizzards were more the norm than the exception. So, why hadn't she listened to the warnings on the radio this morning? Because, like everyone else, she had become complacent, lulled into thinking that the mild winter Denver had thus far enjoyed heralded an early spring. She should have remembered that budding lilacs and the early arrival of yellow and black evening grosbeaks did not guarantee the end of winter.

Almost as if to mock her forgetfulness, large snowflakes began to fall lazily from the sky to plop in ever-increasing numbers against the windscreen of her car. A large gust of wind shook the car, almost jerking the steering-wheel from her grasp. By the time she reached the highway junction at Franktown, the blowing snow was blurring her visibility and she debated whether to go north through Parker or to take the interstate back to Denver. Another severe gust of wind decided her. The old highway through Parker was developed on both sides of the road most of the way. If she did get stuck out in this weather, she wanted to be near civilisation. Turning north on eighty-three, she crept along the road, gritting her teeth as an oncoming car slid by perilously close to her. Right now the roads were wet and slushy, but if the temperature dropped much more, they would quickly turn to treacherous ice.

Leaning over the steering-wheel, Erin peered into the blinding whiteness ahead of her. She couldn't tell if it was still snowing or if the wind was blowing the existing snow. Thank goodness there was little traffic on the two-way road for her to worry about. As it was, she could only guess where the edges of the highway were. The wind died away momentarily and, in the few seconds of visibility Erin was granted, the sign for Merry's subdivision loomed out of the white. Merry's house. Of course. She would drive there and beg shelter from the storm. Merry wouldn't mind. In this part of the country, sanctuary was freely given even to perfect strangers on days like this.

Cautiously Erin executed the wide turn into the area. The wind howled loudly outside the tightly closed car windows. Erin could see trees bent almost to the ground by the force of the storm. The snow crunched beneath the tyres of her car, and she mentally crossed her fingers that no one would come down the steep hill towards her, as she was in the middle of the road and had no wish to end up in the ditch this close to shelter. Rounding the corner, she breathed a sigh of relief at the sight of the Robertses' home. Even as she was slowing up to pull into their driveway, a sense of disquiet stole over her. She didn't have time to wonder about it, however, as almost immediately she realised she was in trouble. The drifting snow in the Robertses' yard had misled her as to the location of the driveway, and the car, suddenly developing a mind of its own, slid gently over the white lawn, coming slowly to rest in a bank of snow higher than her bumpers. Erin sat back in disgust. If she had run over Merry's new flower bed, Merry would have her head. At least she was off the road.

Stepping out from the car disclosed the full power of the blizzard. The wind nearly whipped the car door from Erin's hand, and she fought to hold it open long enough to grab her bag. Head bowed against the snow, she trudged to the front door. It was strange no one had heard her drive up. The entryway provided a small measure of relief from the wind and snow, and Erin stamped her feet thankfully as she pressed the doorbell. The ringing peals echoed inside the house. Then it struck Erin what had bothered her when she had driven up. There was no light in the windows. Even though it wasn't officially dusk, the storm had blocked out the sun and if there were anyone home, they would have the electric lights on.

Erin eyed her footsteps across the lawn. The deep holes were already rapidly filling with snow. With a sigh of resignation, she trudged back to her car. Only a cursory glance was needed to tell her that she wasn't going anywhere until the snow melted unless someone towed her out. Fighting the wind, she managed to open the front door of the car and crawl inside out of the storm. She had better wait in the car until Merry and Neal returned. She hoped they wouldn't be long.

Thirty minutes later she turned off the ignition of her car again. She had only dared run it for a few minutes at a time to warm up the car. Not only was she low on petrol, but dire stories about people asphyxiating in their cars during snow storms kept circulating in her memory. She stamped her wet feet on the floor and hugged herself tightly. Insufficiently dressed for a blizzard, she had been left soaking by her fruitless quest for shelter. Where were the Robertses?

Outside the storm continued to rage. Inside the car, condensation on the windows blotted out what little daylight remained. Rubbing a peep-hole on the window, Erin wondered if she ought to get out and try to walk to one of Merry's neighbours. They would take her in even if they had never met. Thirty more minutes, she decided. If someone didn't show up at the Robertses' house in thirty more minutes, then she would make a run for another house. Shivering she concentrated on the clock on the dashboard.

The knock at the window was totally unexpected. Through the misty windows Erin could make out the outlines of a face staring in at her. Apprehensively she rolled the window down a small space.

'Bird-watching?' Tony's amused voice smoked in the cold air. Erin thought she had never been so glad to see anyone in her life.

'I'm looking for snow geese,' she retorted. Her spirits lightened now that rescue was at hand. The Robertses must have come home without her seeing them, and Tony was obviously with them.

His next statement erased that notion. 'If you're waiting for Merry, the whole family is out of town.'

'No,' Erin wailed. 'They can't be. I'm stuck in their front garden.'

'So I see. Nevertheless, they are. Come on.' He reached in and unlocked her door. 'Let's go.'

'Where?' Erin asked breathlessly as he hauled her from her car, giving her no opportunity to resist.

'To my place. Sorry I couldn't stop when I drove by and saw you, but on this steep hill, I'd never have got my car started again. I honked when I saw you sitting here, but I wasn't sure if you heard me.'

'I didn't.' She pulled back from Tony's grasp. 'I can't go to your place.'

'Don't be stupid.' Tony threw a heavy parka over her shoulders and drew her against his body. He moved away from the car, propelling her irresistibly along with him. 'Now how did I know you'd be too dumb to have a decent winter coat with you?' Sarcasm coated his words.

Erin didn't care as she blissfully snuggled deep into the warmth of his heavy garment. Fighting the wind as they headed up the hill took all her strength. She would argue with Tony later.

The two blocks seemed like two miles. At Tony's house she dropped thankfully on to the bench just inside the door.

Tony lifted his coat from her shoulders. 'A hot bath first,' he said, 'then some dry clothes and something hot to eat.'

'Sounds heavenly,' Erin meekly agreed, which only went to show how much the storm had demoralised her.

Grateful for the warmth and shelter of Tony's house, it wasn't until Erin was soaking in his enormous bathtub that the dangers of her situation struck her, and she began to have doubts about the wisdom of her coming here. Why hadn't she gone

to one of the neighbours when she had a chance?
Then she wouldn't be snowed in with a man noted
for his predatory instincts. Quickly Erin glanced at
the bathroom door. Stupid. She hadn't even locked
it. Footsteps sounded beyond the door, and sinking
beneath the water, she braced herself. There was a
knock on the door.

'I found some jeans that Allie left behind. They
should fit you. I put them on the bed with a sweatshirt of mine,' Tony said from the other side. 'Need
anything else?'

'No, thanks.' Erin waited suspensefully until his
footsteps faded away, releasing her pent-up breath
gratefully. At least Tony had no intention of seducing her in his bathtub. Her mind raced as she
soaked. Tony was an athlete. Surely she could count
on his sense of fair play. Staying in the bathtub as
long as she could, Erin put off the moment when
she had to face Tony again. Had he realised how
thoroughly she was in his power?

Tony looked up as she stood indecisively in the
kitchen doorway. A big grin was quickly smothered.
'Guess that sweatshirt is a little larger than I
realised.'

'What makes you say that?' Erin held out her
arms as she spoke, the sleeve ends drooping at least
a foot beyond her hands.

Tony laughed as he walked over to her. 'Here.'
Reaching for her right arm, he rolled the sleeve up
past her wrist. 'That better?' he asked, as he tackled
the other sleeve.

'Yes.' Having Tony standing so near made Erin
nervous. The memory of him kissing her in this
room flashed into her mind, and her pulse began
to pound. Barely allowing him to finish, she jerked

her arm from his grasp and edged away. 'Thank you for the clothes,' she said primly.

Effortlessly Tony grabbed her and pulled her up against his chest, holding her so close she could barely breathe. Her mind was a jumble of thoughts. She wanted to struggle but feared that opposition would provoke him into actions she didn't want to think about.

'You're at my mercy now,' he said as dark hooded eyes mercilessly studied her face. 'Are you worried?'

'Should I be?' she countered defensively.

'I could pick you up and carry you up to my room and have my way with you, and never even have to breathe hard.' His voice was a menacing growl in Erin's ears. 'You might even enjoy it.'

'I wouldn't,' Erin croaked. He was right about one thing. He was much too strong for her.

Tony laughed harshly, releasing Erin at the same time. 'Well, we'll never know. Because, believe it or not, Miss Cassidy, rape and pillage are not on the agenda for this evening.'

Erin took a deep breath. 'I never thought they were.'

'The hell you didn't. You walked into this kitchen looking like a woman expecting the very worst. As much as I hate to ruin that wonderful image you've built up of me, I have to admit that I only bed willing women. Scared little girls who are forced to seek shelter from the storm in my house don't interest me. You couldn't be safer if you were in church.'

'I wasn't worried.' She took a deep breath. 'After all, aren't athletes supposed to be renowned for their good sportsmanship? I naturally assumed you would play fair.'

Tony hooted derisively. 'What you naturally assumed is that I would resume where we left off the last time you were in this kitchen.'

A warm flush crept up her neck, betraying her. She chose her words carefully. 'What happened before was due to a misunderstanding. Now that you know how I feel, I'm sure it won't happen again.'

'Are you? Is that why you moved across the room, carefully putting the table between us?'

She had hoped he wouldn't notice. 'I . . . I'm just looking for your phone,' she finally stammered.

'Not many people keep their phones in the sink.'

'Sink? Oh,' she said, understanding as the countertop stopped her backward movement and she turned to see the sink behind her.

Tony's face was alight with laughter at her predicament. Erin's fears were shoved aside by the growing suspicion that she was making a fool of herself. 'Where's your darn phone?' she snapped, suddenly out of patience with Tony's little games. Rescuing her from the storm didn't give him the right to laugh at her. 'I need to call my family,' she said coldly. 'They'll be worried.' She bit her lip as a new thought struck her. How in the world was she going to explain this situation to her parents?

'Already done,' Tony said airily. 'I called while you were in the tub. Your dad had just got home, so he knew what the road conditions were. He was relieved to find that you had enough good sense to come to my house.'

Erin flushed. 'Did you explain about the Robertses?'

'And ruin my reputation for having a magnetic appeal for all the ladies?' he asked reproachfully.

Erin refused to be drawn. 'What did my mother say?'

'She said she hoped you'd got out of your wet clothes, and if I don't have rugs, I'm not supposed to let you run around in your bare feet. You catch cold easily.'

'She didn't say that,' Erin disputed weakly, dying inside at what she realised was probably a word-for-word rendition of her mother's remarks.

'I swear, on my mother's grave.'

'Your mother is still alive.'

'Well, if she weren't . . .' Tony held out his hand. 'I think it's time for a truce.'

Erin eyed him doubtfully. 'What kind of truce?'

'What a suspicious person you are,' Tony complained. 'As long as we're snowed in together, I'll treat you just like I treat Allie, and you can pretend that I'm one of your brothers.'

'I suppose that means that you'll try to boss me around and expect me to do all the work.'

'Of course. And like Allie, you'll tell me to go fly a kite.'

Erin laughed, suddenly confident that she had nothing to fear from him. 'If you promise that I can tell you to go fly a kite, it's a deal.'

'I promise,' Tony said solemnly, his hand over his heart. 'Now you'd better call your mom up and reassure her that you're OK. I'm not sure that she believed me. There's a phone by my bed.'

Erin smiled to herself as she dialled her home number. Maybe Tony wasn't quite as bad as she had imagined him. A hand pressed down on the phone button before she could complete her dialling. She looked up in surprise at Tony standing there.

'Before you talk to your mom, put these on.' He dangled a pair of wool socks before her. 'I wouldn't want her to think she couldn't trust her little girl with me,' he added virtuously.

As if cold feet were all her mother had to worry about with Tony, Erin thought in wry amusement.

Cold feet were exactly what her mother was worried about. Putting down the phone after a long conversation with her mother that dealt solely with Erin's health, Erin joined Tony in the kitchen. Heavenly smells wafted from the pot he was vigorously stirring on the stove.

'Well?' Tony demanded. 'Did Carolyn predict dire and dark happenings?'

'Only if I go barefoot,' Erin confessed.

'See. Not everyone sees me as Jack the Ripper.'

'I don't,' Erin protested.

Tony raised a sceptical brow.

'You have to admit that you came on pretty strong,' she insisted.

'A pretty girl like you should be used to men who want to get to know her better.'

'I didn't think getting to know me had anything to do with it,' Erin said drily. 'Unless, of course, you mean strictly in the physical sense. Somehow, picking my brain didn't seem to be your first concern.'

'Touché. I suppose if I added that pretty girls don't need brains, you'd find that offensive.'

'You only need add that an ability to cook is a woman's most important asset to win my undying enmity.'

'You can't cook?' he asked in mock disbelief.

'Let's just say that I'm better with a lead knife than I am with a bread knife.'

CHAPTER FOUR

'WHAT'S a lead knife?' Tony asked. 'That miniature scimitar that you use?'

Erin nodded. 'I admit that I keep it sharp, but it's not exactly a deadly weapon.'

'How did you get started in glass work?' Tony wanted to know.

'Really through a lot of coincidences. Growing up, I spent a lot of time at my grandmother's house—my mother's mother. She lived in one of those huge Victorians over on Capitol Hill. A wonderful old house with overstuffed velvet furniture, lots of dark panelling and a marvellous central staircase. Glass-fronted cabinets and table tops were filled with dusty, fascinating objects. I would sink down on the sofas or hide in the dark corners and pretend I was in some mysterious place, far, far away. The house may have been dark and musty, but to me, every visit there was an adventure. My very favourite place was a small nook on one of the staircase landings that was lighted by a large stained-glass window. I would sit there for hours, fascinated by the patterns the sun and the coloured glass made on the walls. Some of the glass was bevelled, and it worked like a prism, making little rainbows up and down the staircase.'

'And so you decided to make windows like that yourself,' Tony concluded.

'No, I never even thought about it. I've always been interested in art—it's as if there were these pictures in my head that wanted out. All during school, there were art lessons in all kinds of media, but none really satisfied me. I was taking art classes at the University, not really knowing where I was headed. Then one day I walked into a stained-glass studio in Boulder, and all the warm and happy memories of my grandmother's house flooded back. I was hooked. I talked them into hiring me part-time, and then later I heard about the opening down in Phoenix. It seemed a heaven-sent opportunity for me to learn all facets of the field, so off I went.'

'Carolyn told me you'd had to quit your job to come home and help out. You must have been upset by that.'

Erin shrugged. 'I suppose I was a little at first, but it didn't seem I had much choice at the time. Now that I have my own studio, however, I'm terribly excited about the direction my career is taking. I'm not only my own boss, I'm also my own designer. There were times in Phoenix when I'd find myself assembling someone else's window.' She smiled wryly at Tony. 'Good for my technique, bad for my ego. This way I'm personally responsible for the entire project, from designing right through to cleaning the finished work.'

As they had talked, Erin had been setting dishes on the table as Tony finished cooking dinner. Now he placed a steaming bowl of chilli in front of her.

'This smells heavenly,' Erin said, dipping her spoon into the red, bubbling mixture. Seconds later she dropped the spoon and clutched her throat. 'Water,' she croaked.

'Guess I should have warned you that I like my chilli hot and spicy,' Tony said contritely. 'Would you rather have something else?'

Erin was too busy gulping down the iced water
he had handed her to answer. The heat in her mouth
subsiding, she glanced sheepishly at Tony. 'No, this
is good. Really, it is,' she insisted at his mocking
look. 'However, I think I'll add a couple of ice
cubes to it, if you don't mind.'

'That's sacrilegious,' Tony protested, but he
handed her the desired ice.

Watered down, the chilli proved to be just as tasty
and much less dangerous, although Erin's eyes still
had a tendency to water. The meal certainly finished the job of warming her up.

Conversation was much easier over dinner than
Erin expected. Tony spoke of his travels in England
and Canada, having lived in the latter country for
a couple of years while he played in the Canadian
football league. His enthusiasm and descriptions
fired Erin with a desire to visit both countries.

'You certainly have travelled a lot,' she said en-
viously. 'And you still do, playing football all over
the country.'

'During the season about all I see of a city is its
airport and its stadium. Between work-outs, curfew
and the game itself, we don't have a lot of time to
spare.'

'Curfew? Grown men being told what time to go
to bed?'

Tony shrugged. 'Some coaches don't believe in
it, some do. Art does. Personally I think that
playing football is just like every other business. To
get ahead, a person has to do his best. And you
can't do your best when you're out carousing
around all night. We owe it to the fans who pay
good money to see us play to be well prepared for
a game. Unfortunately, not all players feel that way,

so that forces the coach to treat us all like little kids.'

'It must wreak havoc on your social life.'

He grinned. 'I just have to make up for it during the off-season.'

'With the likes of Jennifer, no doubt,' Erin said pertly.

'Jennifer?' Tony frowned in puzzlement. 'Oh, my date at Merry's party. I can't believe you remembered her name.'

'I can't believe you didn't. But I suppose to a man like you, it's not worth the bother to remember their names.'

'What's that supposed to mean?'

'You obviously have so many women waiting in line for a chance to hop into your bed that you can't even put names to their faces.'

'Do you go to bed with every man you're seen in public with?'

'Of course not.'

'Then why do you persist in thinking that I do?'

'Oh, come on, Tony. I read the papers. As my mother always says, there's no smoke without fire.'

'Just because I take a woman out to dinner, doesn't mean that I expect her to stay for breakfast. Believe me, I score a lot more on the field than I do off the field, no matter what the newspapers have to say. Half that stuff in the papers comes directly from the women I date. They like to read about themselves. Jennifer, for example, wants to make it in the television business. She thought I might be a short-cut.'

Erin frowned. 'Doesn't it ever bother you that it's not you they're dating, but the famous Tony Hart?'

'No. It's safer that way. No worry about in
volvement. As long as I have a pretty girl on my
arm to maintain my image, why should I care why
she's there?'

'I think that's sad.'

'You think that's sad because you are obviously
the type that believes in meaningful relationships
leading to marriage. Marriage is not high on my
list of priorities right now.'

'Nothing but a good-time Charlie, in fact,' Erin
mocked.

'That's right. I'm only thirty years old. I've never
heard anything said about a man's biological clock
running out. There's plenty of time for me to settle
down with a wife and family.'

'And a dog. Don't forget a dog.'

Tony laughed, disclosing white, even teeth. 'You
read that, did you? You'd be surprised at how many
women I date these days who profess to be dog-
lovers.'

'I don't think I'd be surprised about anything
concerning the women you date.'

'Methinks I hear a note of pique in that
comment.'

'Not on your life.' She slanted a look at him from
under lowered lashes. 'I'm sorry. Have I bruised
your ego again?'

He slid his chair back from the table. 'You have
to admit you're pretty brutal to the shining knight
who seems to spend his life rescuing you.'

'Aren't you exaggerating a little? One little stroll
in the snow hardly constitutes a lifetime of rescue
operations.'

'How quickly you forget. How about the time I
chased off those drunken college kids who were
harassing you?' he reminded her.

'Oh, that. They were just high-spirited. They wouldn't have done anything.'

'They were high on spirits all right. Instead of following you, I probably should have stuck with them to make sure they didn't cause any other trouble. It makes me furious when I see kids abusing alcohol. Not only are they risking their lives, but they endanger every other person on the road. You can talk, you can show them statistics, but sometimes I just don't know how to reach them.'

'Nicky said that you spend a lot of time trying,' Erin said.

Tony shrugged. 'I guess you could say it's my soapbox. I'll talk to any group that will listen. I'm on one panel that goes around and speaks at schools. There's one guy who totally hit bottom before he quit drugs, and his graphic descriptions can really give you cold chills. Then there's a young man who lost his best friend in a drunken driving accident and a teenage girl who's on parole for killing a small child while driving after popping some pills. Hopefully, their stories will make the kids who are listening stop and think.'

'Where do you fit in on the panel?'

'I try to point out that there are other ways to get your highs. Go hiking in the mountains, develop hobbies, or get involved with sports.'

'Sports! That's like sending an alcoholic to a bar,' Erin pointed out.

'How so?'

'Read the papers. Day after day some noted sports figure is picked up for drunken driving or drug abuse.'

'Your mistake is in blaming the sport for their downfall. That's the excuse they try to make, but it won't wash with me. You can find drunks and addicts in the medical profession, the business world, even among the clergy. Playing football doesn't make a man abuse drugs or alcohol. That man would do it whatever career he chose. Maybe the sudden wealth gives him easier access to drugs, I don't know. I do know that people who have been blessed with special talents, whether it's for football or for acting, owe it to their fans to be a positive role model. Hero-worship makes me uncomfortable, but by the same token, if I can influence one kid to say no to drugs, I'll put up with it.'

There was no mistaking the sincerity in Tony's voice. Thinking over his words, Erin silently helped him clear the dishes from the table.

'It's early yet,' Tony changed the subject. 'Would you like to watch TV, or how about a game of Scrabble? I even have some game films,' he said, a mischievous glint in his eyes.

'Scrabble,' Erin chose quickly. It was the wrong choice. 'How could I have forgotten that you were a Rhodes scholar?' she asked mournfully several hours later. 'I used to pride myself on my ability to play this game. I'll never have a swelled head again.'

'You needn't feel so badly,' Tony counselled in a teasing voice. 'The only reason I humiliated you is because I'm so much smarter.'

'That's what I like. A generous winner,' Erin said drily. She leaned back against the sofa that they were sharing and rubbed the kink in her neck. Three hours of intense concentration combined with bending over the low table before them had left her muscles protesting.

'Here. Let me.' Tony pulled her closer to him and began kneading her tired muscles.

His fingers knew all the right moves, and the protest she had been about to make died in her throat. 'Ummm. That feels good.' Her eyes closed, she sat there silently, becoming limp under Tony's healing massage. When his touch softened and he pushed her chin up, giving him access to her lips, she went into his embrace obediently, her body boneless in his arms.

At first his lips were cool and somewhat aloof against hers, but when she didn't draw back, Tony deepened the kiss sending delicious shivers through her body. She snuggled closer to him, and somehow the two of them slid lower on the couch until she was lying beneath him. Erin felt Tony draw back and she knew he was watching her face, but she refused to open her eyes. Rough thumbs traced her lips to be followed by the moist ministrations of his tongue. Fingers pressed at the corners of her mouth, persuaded her lips to part, allowing his tongue to tenderly probe and caress. The taste of coffee clung to his mouth.

Tentatively Erin curled her tongue around his, catching her breath at the sharp burst of sensation which derived from this simple action. A low moan of pleasure from Tony intensified her own enjoyment and gave her a heady sense of power. Bolder now, she allowed her tongue free reign in exploring the moist inner recesses of Tony's mouth, all the while revelling in the unfamiliar but agreeable feelings that pervaded her limbs.

Then his hands cupped her face, holding it still as he reminded her who was the master and who was the novice. Shaken by the sensations that flowed through her veins, Erin twisted on the sofa, drawing Tony's attention to the rest of her body. Searching hands exploring the front of her body reminded her that her underwear was drying over the shower rod in Tony's bathroom. The thought was only fleeting, however, as Tony's hands slid under the voluminous sweatshirt and glided over her heated skin, arousing waves of sensation that were so intensely pleasureful that Erin knew she could feel no more. She was wrong. Tony pushed the sweatshirt up, and his murmured words of appreciation were as sensuous as a warm touch, before the feel of his lips suckling the sensitive tips of her breasts drove all coherent thought from her mind. Turning her head, she licked the rough, salty skin of his arm. A faint residue of his aftershave mingled with the warm scent of his body and filled her nostrils.

Tony lifted his body from hers, leaving Erin feeling cold and abandoned. 'I think it's time we went to bed,' he said huskily.

Erin's eyes widened in horror, only to close again in order to block out the disturbing light in his. 'No, I...I...'

'Before you say any more,' Tony coolly interrupted her, 'I meant to separate beds.'

Erin's eyes snapped open. Tony was watching her with an intent blue gaze. If there had been desire in his eyes a moment ago, it had totally vanished now. She pulled the sweatshirt back into place, slowly smoothing out the wrinkles as she sought desperately for something to say. No words came to her rescue.

'As much as I've enjoyed this delightful interlude, I've a very strong suspicion that you're a virgin, and believe me, I have no interest in virgins. Too dangerous. Virgins are the bait for a trap that I have no intention of being caught in.'

Erin shot upright on the sofa. 'Is that what you think? That I'm trying to seduce you into my bed so that you'll have to marry me?'

Tony laughed shortly. 'I don't think you're clever enough for that.'

'Thank you very much. That's twice in the last hour you've called me stupid,' Erin said bitterly.

He reached over and twined a springy black curl around his fist, studying Erin through narrowed lids. 'Maybe I should have said you're not experienced enough. Are you disappointed?' he asked as she shook her hair loose from his grasp.

Erin gasped at the sheer effrontery of his question. Her voice shook with anger as she answered him. 'Going to bed with you does not happen to be one of my major aspirations in life.'

Tony shrugged. 'Your loss.'

'You are absolutely the most arrogant, egotistical male I . . . I ever . . . ever met!' Erin sputtered.

Tony stood up, addressing her harshly over his solid shoulder. 'Run back to your friend Martin. You don't belong in the major league. You're out of your depth here.'

'I never wanted to be in your league. You don't play fair. A truce you said, and I believed you. I trusted you.'

'You shouldn't have,' Tony said coldly. 'A woman as beautiful as you has no business trusting any man.'

'What a cynical outlook on life you have,' she cried.

'Not cynical. Just realistic.'

'If that's your idea of reality, I'm glad that I am in a different league from yours. I wouldn't want any part of a world where people are so callous, so uncaring, so. . . .'

Tony cut her off in a voice weary of listening to her indictments. 'I put clean sheets on my bed while you were in the bathtub. If you'll look in the bottom drawer on the right side of the wardrobe, you'll find some pyjamas that I received for Christmas a couple of years ago. They've never been worn.'

'I wouldn't want to put you out of your bed,' Erin said stiffly.

'Assuming that's not an invitation to join you there, I'll sleep in the basement. I'm going to work out for a while and the exercise-room is right next door to the guest bedroom.'

Knowing that further protest was fruitless, Erin quickly went up the stairs to Tony's bedroom. She found the pyjamas where he had said they would be and spared a thought for whoever would buy him maroon silk trimmed in pink. The bottoms were impossibly large, but the top dropped to her knees, giving her plenty of protection. Protection. What an odd choice of word. Why would she possibly need protection?

From far below came the sounds of machinery squeaking and thumping. An exercise bicycle, or perhaps weights, Erin guessed. She slid into bed and huddled beneath the covers, unable to sleep, her mind replaying again and again the recent scene enacted on the sofa. She could find no excuses for her own behaviour. Yes, she had been tired. Yes, she had had an unpleasant experience, and yes, Tony had rescued her. And yes, he had fed her and entertained her, and she had enjoyed the evening. None of that explained how she had ended up half-naked on the sofa making love with a man she detested for his lack of moral fibre.

Honesty forced her to temper that thought. Admittedly Tony's amorous dealings could best be compared to those of a roving tomcat, but there was another side to him. His courtesies to her parents, his apparently close and loving relationship with his own family. His sincere concerns about drugs and alcohol abuse combined with his efforts to combat the problem. Clearly there was more to Tony than his macho reputation as a jock and a stud indicated.

The truth was, Tony was a enigma to her. He seemed to be a thoughtful, caring person in every instance except one: dealing with women. Of course, he implied that he only dated women who knew the score, but Erin wondered how much of that was true and how much he merely assumed was true. There was no denying that Tony was good-looking, charming, talented, amusing—not to mention famous—in fact, at times, a positive paragon among men. It certainly wouldn't stretch the imagination to suppose that among the many women he dated, some must have been rash enough to fall in love with him.

Maybe not. Maybe there was some kind of aura that people like Tony gave off that attracted those of the same ilk and repelled all others. Certainly he had never lied about his intentions to her. Not that she wanted him to have any intentions about her one way or the other. Which of course, led her back to her initial question. Why did she keep ending up in the arms of a man she didn't even like very much? What was there about him that attracted her at the same time as she was repelled by his profession and his playboy mentality?

Her thoughts wandered to Martin who embodied all the characteristics she sought in a man. Intelligent, sensitive; his interests complemented hers. When Martin took her out, they were likely to attend a symphony concert or a gala exhibit opening. He shared her love of art, and their Sunday afternoons spent browsing through museums and galleries were warm and companionable. He treated her to intimate little dinners and lunches where they discussed politics and world affairs. She approved of his all-white apartment, the perfect background for his stunning and colourful collection of modern art. Martin and his wallet both favoured young, undiscovered artists who he was sure were the Picassos of the future. Erin had no doubt that his instincts were reliable; she had enjoyed the hunt for such art and been thrilled by Martin's discoveries as much as he had. As a couple they were undeniably compatible, with innumerable common bonds and shared enthusiasms.

Except when Martin kissed her. No bells went off, no earth moved. Erin's heart beat no faster, her breathing remained regular. She flopped over on her stomach in disgust. She wasn't being fair to Martin. He didn't begin to have the experience that Tony had. Certainly Martin had never fondled her breasts. Why not? Erin turned to lie on her back, staring at Tony's wooden ceiling. He respected her, of course. Or, you don't make any bells ring for him either, a little voice whispered.

The noise coming up from the basement had ceased. The unwelcome image of a bare-chested Tony, warm and sweating from his work-out, invaded Erin's thoughts. She tried to thrust the picture from her mind, conjuring up instead the memory of the latest painting that Martin was considering purchasing. She disliked the painting. It was too bland for her. Beige, browns, blond. Tony's chest hairs were blond. Erin rolled over and buried her face in her pillow. Could it possibly be that she, who prided herself on her admiration of cerebral skills instead of brawn, had fallen for a fabulous set of pectoral muscles?

The next morning found Erin no nearer to understanding her conflict about Tony. The only thing she knew was that she couldn't like a man like him. She would chalk her momentary lapses in his arms up to experience, or inexperience, more likely. As a result of her mixed feelings, she was cold and distant to Tony at the breakfast table. At the same time, he was in a foul mood, slamming around dishes and snapping at her few comments. Apparently a night of celibacy didn't agree with him.

After breakfast, over Tony's objections, Erin joined him outside in shovelling the snow from the driveway. The entire neighbourhood was white and pristine, unmarked by tyre treads or footprints. As they shovelled, the huge piles of snow seemed incongruous in the April sunshine. They had almost finished clearing the walks and drive when a huge yellow snowplough charged by, spewing behind a fan-shaped trail that partially negated their hard work. With a muttered curse, Tony cleared the drive a second time.

Speaking to Erin only to issue terse commands, they drove down to her car, where, with the aid of extensive shovelling and a stout chain attached between her car and Tony's second car, a small station wagon with front-wheel drive, they managed to pull her car out into the ploughed roadway.

'I'll follow you home,' Tony yelled out of his open window.

'Thank you, but that won't be necessary,' Erin said stiffly. She had endured enough of his pouting. Had he expected a tangible demonstration of her gratitude last night? He was the one who sent her off to bed alone.

Of course Tony ignored her refusal to have him follow her. When did he ever listen to her opinion? Erin fumed. She crept cautiously out of the housing area, gaining more confidence when she arrived at the highway and saw that traffic and the morning sun had already completely cleared the road of snow. Beside the road, cars and trucks parked haphazardly in snow banks told the story of the unexpected fury of the spring storm. She hadn't been the only traveller forced to seek sanctuary last night.

In spite of the benevolent road conditions, Tony insisted on dogging her trail all the way to her home. Erin's temper began to rise. The sooner she saw the last of Tony Hart, the better. In spite of all logic and reasoning, she continually betrayed herself in his presence. There was something about him that melted her resistance to his type. That shouldn't surprise her. A man didn't gain a reputation like Tony's by being the kind of man that women could easily resist. And she admitted it. He tempted her. His winning smile, his entertaining charm. The man was potent medicine. Snake-oil medicine, she thought. Only an illusion.

As she turned into her driveway she welcomed the sight of Martin striding briskly from her house. Coming to a stop beside him, she eagerly opened the car door. 'Martin, I thought you were in Chicago.'

'Obviously,' he sneered, his nostrils flared in contempt.

Erin stepped from the car, frowning at his unexpected behaviour. 'Is something the matter?'

Martin looked over her shoulder at Tony who had just driven up and was getting out of his car.

'Did you think since I was in Chicago I wouldn't find out? Unluckily for you, I finished up a day early and came home today instead of tomorrow as I'd anticipated.' He glared at them both. A glimpse of hurt surfaced momentarily beneath his anger.

'It's wonderful that you're back early,' Erin began, uncertain why he appeared to be so irate.

'I thought I could trust you,' he spat out. 'The last person on earth...' Anger choked off his words.

'Martin, what are you talking about?' Erin felt as if she had entered in the middle of a bad movie.

'I think he's accusing you of lascivious behaviour.' Tony's voice from behind her was laced with amusement.

Martin stiffened at Tony's mocking words. 'You may have convinced Erin's parents that her spending the night at your house was a genuine emergency, but don't expect me to fall for that excuse. I have eyes. I can see how clear the roads are. You can't expect me to believe that it was impossible for Erin to make it home from Parker last night.'

'That's exactly what I expect you to believe.' The amusement was gone from Tony's voice. It was hard-edged and implacable.

Martin ignored Tony's remark, turning to Erin. 'A woman as beautiful as you and an acknowledged sex-fiend. I knew the first time I saw him at your house that he had only one plan with regard to you, to get you into his bed. I suppose you can't be blamed. You're not in his league.'

Erin swallowed a hysterical giggle. Was she wearing a sign? The world's most inexperienced virgin? What little amusement that thought afforded her must have been reflected on her face, because Martin's eyes grew black with fury.

'Does it amuse you that I'm upset at the thought of your sleeping with someone else?'

'No, no. Martin, it doesn't. I didn't. We didn't. You're wrong,' Erin stammered, stunned by Martin's mistaken accusations.

'Are you trying to tell me that you spent the night at *his* house and he didn't share your bed, didn't make passionate love to you, kissing you until you were putty in his arms? Can you stand there and tell me that?'

Erin just looked at him. At Martin's words about kisses, she felt a warm flush crawl up her neck, and the guilt on her face betrayed her.

'You tramp!' Martin slapped her hard across her face.

Tony moved so fast that Erin barely saw him through eyes blurred with pain from Martin's unexpected violence. Blinking the tears from her eyes she saw Martin lying on the ground rubbing his jaw while Tony stood over him, a blaze of anger on his face.

'Don't you ever touch Erin again,' Tony ground out through clenched teeth.

Doyle Cassidy erupted from the house. 'My God!' he breathed. 'I couldn't believe it when I saw him hit Erin. What kind of person are you?' He looked with disgust at Martin, still supine on the ground, before encircling Erin's shaking shoulders with a comforting arm.

Erin remembered little of what happened next. She was delivered into her mother's soothing care, an ice-pack placed on her burning cheek. At some point in time, both Martin and Tony left. She didn't care if she never saw either of them again. How could Martin trust her so little? Was he far wrong? a little voice persisted in asking. Tony was the one who prevented anything from happening, not her.

Martin called the next day in remorse, but Erin refused to hear him out. A man who would hit her once could lose his temper and do it again. She wanted nothing more to do with him.

To Nicky's chagrin, the incident also spelled the end of Tony's dropping in for Sunday dinner or to toss the football around with Nicky and his friends.

'I don't blame you,' he assured his sister as they sat on the old porch swing on a warm early May evening watching a solitary water-skier skimming across Sloan Lake. 'How could you know that old Martin was going to turn out to be such a creep? I'm sure Tony doesn't want to come over here just in case Martin decides to get ugly again.'

'Tony is twice the size of Martin. I doubt he's afraid of him,' Erin said drily.

'Use your head, Erin. Martin could do a lot of damage to Tony's character by spreading gossip about him. Seducing an innocent young woman and assaulting her fiancé when he protested.'

'In the first place, Tony did not seduce me. Nothing happened at his house. In the second place, he did not assault Martin, nor was Martin ever my fiancé.'

'I know that. But would everyone reading it in the paper believe it? Look at you. You believe all that dirt you read about Tony,' he added shrewdly.

'I do not.'

'You've had a grudge against Tony ever since that little accident.'

'It wasn't a little accident to me,' Erin cried. 'Besides, I don't blame him for the accident, not really. He shouldn't have let an inexperienced person drive such a powerful car, but I can understand that. What irritates me is that he never felt the least bit badly about it. Losing Mrs Filmore's business was a big blow to me. He might have shown some concern for my feelings.'

'He commissioned a window, didn't he?'

Erin stared at her younger brother. 'What's that got to do with anything?'

Nicky shrugged. 'I always thought it was his way of making amends. You blamed him for closing down one avenue for you, so he tried to open up another. Jeez, Erin. Couldn't you figure that out for yourself?'

'No,' she said slowly. 'I thought he was...was, well, you know.'

'Putting the moves on you? Don't think much of yourself, do you? Tony has his pick of women. Why would he waste time on you?'

'Thanks,' Erin said drily. 'Every girl should have a brother to keep her from getting a swelled head.'

'Ah, you know what I mean. You're OK for a sister, and I know some of my friends practically drool when you come into the room, but face it, Erin. Tony is Tony Hart. You're, you're...'

'Yes?'

'You're my sister!' he blurted out.

'For my sins,' Erin dramatically intoned. She reached over and tousled Nicky's hair. 'I'll remember this conversation when the girls start coming around for you,' she threatened.

'Never.' Hearing their mother call him to the phone, Nicky went into the house.

Leaving Erin disturbed by his comments. She slowly pushed the swing back and forth with her toe, thinking about what Nicky had said. The thought that Tony had hired her to make reparation had never occurred to her. Now that she thought about it, Tony had suggested that making a window for him might help her business. Although it was true, she had discounted that as his genuine motive. Nicky's startling conclusion wasn't one that gave her joy. She preferred to paint Tony strictly in terms of black and white, mostly black. She certainly didn't want to be in any way beholden to him.

Nicky reappeared in the doorway. 'That was Tony on the phone. He wanted to know how I'd done on the history test he helped me study for last week.'

'How did you do?'

'Aced it. Tony had some neat ideas on how I could remember the dates.' He added casually, 'He wanted to know how his window is coming along. I told him to come over tomorrow and see for himself.' He shot Erin a quick glance. 'Hope you've been working on it.'

'Fret not, kiddo. Your sister has had her nose to the grindstone. Or, her glass to it, at any rate,' she said gaily, trying to ignore the nervous churnings of her stomach at Nicky's announcement. Between her abandoned behaviour in Tony's arms the night of the blizzard and Martin's atrocious behaviour the next morning, she wasn't sure if she could face Tony again. His non-appearance had been a relief to her, torn as she was between the desire never to see him again, and the growing awareness that his window was going to be good, very good, and she wouldn't be able to bear the thought of its collecting dust in her workshop for years to come.

Her nerves were no calmer the next day as she worked on Tony's window. Accepting Tony's commission had been a mistake. What should be purely a business relationship kept developing other aspects that she preferred not to think about. In every encounter with Tony the firm foundation beneath her feet rapidly turned out to be quicksand. Belatedly she wished she had invented an excuse to be anywhere else when Tony arrived. He didn't need her to see what she had done. Engrossed in her thoughts, she was unaware of Tony's arrival until he spoke.

'What are you doing?' he asked, frowning over her shoulder at the work in progress.

Startled, Erin jumped, dropping her roll of foil to the floor. 'I didn't hear you come in,' she said, avoiding his eyes.

Tony picked up the roll. 'What's this?'

'Copper foil. For your window.'

'That's not what you were doing to the window I saw you working on before.'

'I was working with lead then, but lead lines would look too thick and heavy for a delicate design like yours,' Erin explained, more than willing to discuss a neutral subject. With luck, Tony wouldn't even bring up the blizzard. She picked up a cut piece of glass and showed him the foil crimped around the edges. 'I'm doing it in copper foil, a technique that Louis Tiffany developed. I wrap each piece with the copper tape. Then when all the pieces are fitted on to the pattern, I'll solder them together.' She stood back from her work bench. 'What do you think?'

Tony carefully scrutinised the glass pieces lying on the work bench. 'I think that I can't tell a thing with it lying on the brown paper.'

'I suppose it is pretty hard to visualise it without the sun shining through the glass so that you can see the true colours.' Uneasily she remembered Nicky's theory that Tony had only ordered a

window to make amends. If Nicky was right, and
Tony didn't care about having a window, then it
was even more important that Tony should fall in
love with this particular window. It wouldn't be
much of an advertisement for her if he hated it.
Besides, as much as she disliked the idea, if the
window was Tony's idea of reparation, then perhaps
she owed him something for her unjust assumptions. She flicked an anxious look in his direction.
'I hope it's what you want.'

Tony leaned back against the work bench and
studied her face. 'I thought you knew what I
wanted,' he drawled softly.

Erin's hands clenched at her side but she refused
to acknowledge the double meaning of his
comment. 'It's not too late to change any of the
glass if any of this doesn't appeal to you.'

Tony shrugged. 'I told you. I'm leaving all that
in your hands.'

'I just want you to be satisfied,' Erin said.

Tony uttered a short laugh. 'I doubt that.'

Erin felt a warm flush crawl up her neck at Tony's
remark. No doubt about his meaning. Why couldn't
she think before she opened her mouth? Picking
up the roll of foil, she concentrated on the window,
hoping that Tony would take the hint and leave.
She might have known he wouldn't.

He strolled around her workshop, pausing now
and then to watch her work. As usual, his presence
seemed to shrink her surroundings. 'Don't you have
something else to do?' she finally asked pointedly.

He lifted his eyebrows. 'Am I bothering you?'

'I don't like anyone staring over my shoulder.'

He lifted a quizzical brow. 'Anyone or me in
particular?'

She put down her tools and glared defiantly at him. 'Anyone.'

Tony reached over and traced her cheekbone with a lazy finger. 'You are the least truthful woman I've ever met. Why are you so afraid to admit that you're attracted to me? I admit that your body turns me every which way but loose.'

Shaken as much by his words as by his touch, Erin said candidly, 'I don't want to be attracted to a man like you. That kind of attraction is like sugar; tastes good, but it's bad for you.'

The teasing look on Tony's face disappeared, and he studied her with shuttered eyes. 'You're probably right.'

Before she could reply to that she heard her mother calling from the house. Tony sauntered to the door.

'Your mom invited me to stay for lunch. Coming?'

For an answer, Erin held up her stained fingers. 'You go ahead. I'll be there in a few minutes.' As his footsteps echoed loudly on the outside staircase, she leaned weakly against the work bench. Sometimes she wished that she were a different kind of woman, one who could ignore her own beliefs about love and marriage. An affair with Tony would be filled with pleasure and ecstasy. She didn't doubt that he was skilled in the ways of making love. He promised excitement. For a short time. The one thing that Tony didn't promise was permanence, and for Erin that was of paramount importance. For her, the act of love was a commitment. For Tony, it was a pleasant way to spend the afternoon.

Sighing she walked over to the sink and washed her hands. There was no point in dwelling on what would never be. Reluctantly she went to lunch.

CHAPTER FIVE

SINCE it was a weekday, only Erin and her mother were at home. With little effort Tony started Carolyn on stories of her family. Erin sighed in resignation at some of the embellishments her mother put on incidents from Erin's past. She knew from experience there was no point in correcting or trying to stop her mother. If Carolyn chose to rewrite history to make that history more interesting, Erin was powerless to stop her. She did wish that Carolyn would get off the subject of Erin's old boyfriends.

'Speaking of old boyfriends, what do you hear from Martin?' Tony turned abruptly to Erin.

'He called to apologise, but I'm not seeing him any more,' she said stiffly. She couldn't believe that she hadn't had a clue that Martin's mild manners hid such a violent temper.

'I was never so mistaken about a person,' Carolyn said in chagrin, echoing Erin's thoughts. 'He seemed so nice, and I was so happy to see Erin having such an enjoyable social life. It was hard for her to leave all her friends and move back here.'

Erin could feel the blood rushing to her face. Her mother made her sound like an old maid whose last hope had been Martin. 'I have other friends here,' she reminded her mother.

Tony stared down at his plate. 'How would you like to go to a party with me Saturday night, Erin?'

'How nice of you to ask her, Tony. She'd love to.'

'Mother!' Erin said in annoyance. 'Will you let me speak for myself?' She didn't want to go out with Tony, and even if she did, she certainly didn't appreciate his asking her because he felt sorry for her. 'I'm . . . I'm already busy,' she answered.

'Doing what?'

'Don't you have any social manners?' Erin demanded. 'When a woman turns you down, you're supposed to accept her rejection gracefully.'

'Erin!' her mother gasped in disbelief.

Tony's lips twisted ironically. 'Meaning you aren't busy, you just don't want to go out with me.'

'I didn't say that,' Erin countered evasively.

'Fine. In that case, I'll pick you up about six-thirty. The party is at my brother's house in Boulder.'

'I never said that I was going . . .'

Tony stood up. 'See you at six-thirty. Thanks for lunch, Carolyn. Delicious, as usual.'

'I'm not going!' Erin shouted after him as he walked out of the door.

Carolyn Cassidy might be able to bring pressure to bear to get Erin to go out with Tony, but she couldn't make her be ready on time. Carolyn had made a big fuss about Erin's refusal. When her mother had said how guilty she felt over Erin's having to move back to Denver, and insisted that it was her fault that Erin's social life was lacking, and finally had resorted to tears, Erin knew the battle was lost.

Resenting her mother's manipulations, Erin had pouted around the house until Saturday finally arrived. She could hear her mother downstairs now chatting with Tony. Fully dressed, Erin pottered around her bedroom, putting off going downstairs. Her twin image stared back at her from the oval cheval mirror in the corner. The loosely cut silk sweatshirt and slacks in a rich navy provided the perfect background for a striking modern necklace of chunky nuggets of silver interspersed with interesting shapes and colours of translucent glass, a collaborative effort between herself and a silversmith friend.

Erin twisted the large matching bracelet cuff around her wrist, watching the minutes click away on her bedroom clock. She wanted to make it perfectly clear to Tony that she was going with him under protest, and left to her own choosing, the last thing she would be doing was going to some dumb party with him. The thought of having to listen to football talk all night was depressing.

She said as much to Tony when he closed the car door behind her.

'Football talk,' he said in surprise. 'What makes you think that?'

'He is your brother, so naturally I assume he's a coach at that school where he teaches.'

'He's my brother which automatically means he's a dumb athlete. I can see that you've already deduced that he's married to a cheerleader, his kids all play on Little League teams, and when you sit down in the bathroom, the seat plays the Nebraska fight song.'

'You made that last part up.'

'You mean that's not what you're expecting?' Tony asked in mocking astonishment.

'All you talk about at my house is football,' she pointed out in her own defence.

'You come from a football-crazy family, I have to admit,' Tony agreed. 'That's why I find it so surprising that you dislike sports so much. Having five brothers, you'd think that you'd be a sports nut just like they are.'

'Having five brothers is exactly why I'm not just like them. When I came along my mom told my dad that he had three sons, and I belonged to her. While the menfolk played ball, or went fishing, Mother was driving me to dance lessons or art shows. Maybe if I'd had a sister, things would have been different, but two more boys after me only made my mother more determined that I was not going to be a tomboy.'

'I've seen all the trophies that your brothers have won lining the shelves. Your mom seems awfully proud of them.'

'Oh, she is. She's not interested in sports, but she's crazy about her boys. She delighted in their victories and suffered through their defeats. Once in a while she even attended their games. Not often, though. With six kids she said she was too busy to watch other people playing.'

'With six kids, I'd have thought she had lots of help around the house.'

'That's where you're wrong. Even when the boys weren't playing a game, they were practising, or lifting weights, or jogging to keep in shape. There was always some activity which stopped them from helping Mom. And all those sports made more work for Mom. No matter what the weather, she'd be out driving them to practice and games before they had their licences. She'd scheme to get them on the same team, but usually unsuccessfully, which doubled and tripled her driving time. And of course, there were all those uniforms to wash.'

'What about your dad?'

'He was the worst of all. Do you know that my mother had to have a neighbour drive her to the hospital when she gave birth to Nicky because he was at an Explorers football game?'

'Surely that was just an accident.'

'Mother warned him that she was sure Nicky was going to come that day, but Daddy was just as sure that he'd be home in time, and besides, my older brothers really wanted to see that game. It goes without saying that the Explorers lost,' she added drily.

Tony grinned. 'Before my time, I'm afraid. I suppose your dad was quite an athlete himself in high school.'

'No, he didn't have a chance to play sports when he was younger because he had to work after school to help out at home. Mom always said that he was re-living his youth through my brothers. Not that they minded. They were all good at sports. I don't want you to get the wrong idea. My mother adores my father, and whatever he wants to do is all right with her. She's perfectly happy with their life. I just want something more than living with a man who's too busy watching you being a hero on television even to notice me.'

Tony laughed. 'Not always the hero, I'm afraid.' He switched back to her family. 'One thing makes me curious. Where did you fit into all this?'

'I didn't. When I was little I had my girlfriends to play with in the neighbourhood, and my own interests. Mom and I shopped and went to movies, and visited museums. It wasn't until I got older that I realised other families did things together. Summers, for example, we couldn't take family holidays because the boys were always off at sports camps, usually all at different times. Christmas meant basketball tournaments. In high school and college, I was involved with drama and the arts, but only Mom came to see the plays or the art shows. There was always a football game or a track meet.'

Tony squinted into the bright setting sun. 'Did you ever give any of their sports a try? I mean, go to any of their games and see if maybe you'd enjoy watching them.'

'Oh, sure.' She added demurely, 'Just as soon as I started noticing boys.'

'It figures. You probably had them standing in line.'

'I did. Unfortunately not for myself. I discovered that the boys were chasing me to get to know my brothers, who had all made names for themselves in various sports. Girls were even worse. Hanging all over me in hopes that I'd introduce them to Kevin or Alan or even Baird, who's two years younger than I am.'

Tony smiled briefly in her direction. 'Poor Erin. You must have hated it.'

'Sometimes I did,' she said candidly. 'That's when I decided that I would never date anyone who was on the football team or the basketball team or who ran track or swam or played golf or any other sport I could think of.'

'That must have wiped out a fair number of candidates,' Tony commented.

'Maybe. But the ones left didn't spend the whole night complaining about curfew or giving me a blow-by-blow description of their last game. I didn't have to pretend to admire flexed muscles or athletic feats.'

'Your dad must think you're a foundling dropped by mistake on his doorstep,' Tony teased.

'That's where you're wrong,' Erin said firmly. 'Girls are supposed to be pretty and pink, not all red-faced and sweaty. He firmly approves that I'm not sports-minded. In fact,' she giggled, 'my brother Rourke's wife played collegiate basketball and is now on a women's softball team. She's another sports nut and can reel off statistics like nobody's business. Daddy is overwhelmed by her, and he never quite knows how to talk to her. He thinks that on Thanksgiving she's supposed to be helping set the table, not watching the big games on TV. She drives him almost as crazy as my brother Kevin. Kevin's the foundling. He was a good athlete, but he is also the kindest, most gentle man, with a beautiful way with words. He's involved with the theatre out on the east coast and hopes to be a playwright, and he will be. I think you met him when he was home a couple of weekends ago. Did he tell you about his latest play?'

'No.' He gave her a wry smile. 'All we talked about was football.'

'There's just so much more to life than sports. I think that's my biggest gripe about athletes. They get so wrapped up in a silly game that they forget that there's another whole world going on around them.'

'Maybe if you tried harder to show interest in their world, they'd appreciate yours more,' Tony pointed out.

'You're just saying that because you're a football player yourself,' Erin retorted. 'Which leads me to something I'm curious about. How did a man smart enough to win a Rhodes scholarship end up playing professional football?'

'Pride and curiosity,' Tony answered promptly.

'If you think that's an answer that will satisfy my curiosity, you're dead wrong.'

'I played ball in high school, but since the school was in a small farming community, my accomplishments didn't rate much press, or interest. Like every other boy who grew up on Cornhusker football games, it was my dream to attend the University of Nebraska. But, I needed a scholarship, and they couldn't see their way to giving me one. Unfortunately, studying hadn't been that important to me, so my grades weren't any help. A small college in eastern Nebraska finally offered me financial aid.' He shrugged. 'It was that or nothing, so I grabbed at the offer. We had a winning season, and the people at U. of N. came to see me, but I'd have had to sit out a year, and by then, I liked the smaller school. There was a Professor Mills there who turned me on to learning. For the first time in my life I didn't study merely to pass a course, but because I wanted to absorb all the knowledge I could. Eventually, that led to the scholarship offer in England.'

'I'm surprised you didn't turn it down to go play football.'

Tony grinned. 'Would you believe that I almost did? What a blow it was to my ego when I didn't get drafted by anyone in the NFL. Playing at a small school, no matter what my statistics were, didn't give me enough credibility. The scouts said I'd never be able to play against the big boys. So I thumbed my nose at them and took off for Oxford.'

'Then how did you get back in football?' Erin asked, confused by Tony's recounting of events.

'As my time in England began winding down, I started to get that old itch. I knew I was good enough to play in the NFL. All I had to do is prove it. Looking around the NFL, I couldn't see that any of those teams were ready to give me a chance, so I took off to Canada and managed to sign on as a free agent up there. Three years and three winning seasons made the people down here take a second look at me. I was drafted back east, but they already had two strong quarterbacks, and I rode the bench for two seasons, begging to be traded. Finally the deal with the Explorers was worked out, so I came to Denver.'

'I still don't understand why you wanted to play football when you had so much potential in other areas,' Erin said.

'If I did have that potential, I still do,' Tony pointed out. 'Football is a young man's sport. I'll play for a few more years, and then I'll think about switching to another career. In the meantime, I'm proving something to myself and to all those doubting Thomases who said I'd never make it in the big league. On top of which, and I know this is hard for you to understand, but I truly love the game. Not just the glamour and the exposure, that's part of it, but for me, it's the game itself. It pushes me to my limits. Am I thinking fast enough, running fast enough, throwing accurately? A hundred different physical and mental skills coming together. A victory that I've helped engineer is like finishing a fine piece of furniture. Doing my best makes me feel good about myself.' He glanced her way. 'There's more to life than art, you know.'

Her own words turned against her. Was Tony accusing her of the same narrow-minded thinking that she attributed to athletes? She decided to ignore his implication. 'Tell me more about your family.'

'What's to tell? You already met my sister Allie. Daniel's a couple of years younger than I am. I think you'll like his wife, Joanna.'

'The cheerleader.'

'Right.'

'Then I won't like her,' Erin said positively. 'Cheerleaders are always vivacious and always insipid.'

'At least you're going with an open mind,' Tony observed drily.

This time there was no doubting his meaning.

Erin wished she could take back the biased remark. Trying to ignore the awkward silence his remark had engendered, she gazed out of the window at the passing landscape. There was the usual heavy traffic around the 'mousetrap', that section of the interstate where so many on-and-off ramps required drivers to be vigilant. Tony capably guided the sports car on to the Boulder turnpike. As they headed west the foothills ahead of them were washed with pink by the setting sun.

Music and laughter spilled from a gaily lit house deep in Coal Creek Canyon as Tony pulled up in the driveway. Erin was out of the car before he had reached her side.

'Just so you know that I think about something besides football, I want you to know that I think you look fabulous tonight,' Tony said, a teasing light in his eyes.

'I've always known you had at least one other interest,' Erin retorted.

Taking her arm, he guided her towards the house. 'You're supposed to say, "Thank you, Tony".'

'Thank you, Tony,' she parroted.

'You don't do that often enough.'

'What? Say thank you?'

'No. Do what you're told.'

Erin was punching him lightly on the arm when the door opened. Her embarrassment was not lessened when Tony immediately asked the freckled, dark blonde woman standing there if she had ever been a cheerleader.

The woman's answering laughter was contagious. 'Heavens, no. Cheerleaders have to be able to walk across the room without tripping over their own feet,' she answered cheerfully. 'Why in the world are you asking?'

'Erin hates cheerleaders,' Tony said, completely destroying Erin's composure.

'So do I. Everyone knows that cheerleaders and baton twirlers are totally bubble-headed,' the woman said firmly. 'Incidentally, since Tony can't be bothered to introduce us, I'm Joanna Hart, and you're?' Her voice rose in interrogation.

'Erin Cassidy.'

Before she could say any more, a man's laughing voice hollered from inside the house. 'Joanna, Dixie heard your remark about cheerleaders and she says she resents it.' The voice was followed up by the appearance of a slighter version of Tony. 'Tony! What's the matter? Won't Joanna let you come in?' Seeing Erin, he immediately loosed a low, fervent whistle. 'Never mind Tony. Who are you?' Crooking his elbow within hers, he pulled Erin into the house. 'Don't tell me that Tony is sharing his ill-gained booty with me at last?'

'Easy to see you're Tony's brother,' Erin teased.

Daniel flicked an imaginary moustache. 'You mean because I'm as wickedly handsome or because I'm just as sexy?'

'I meant you're just as outrageous a flirt.'

'Do I detect a wee hint that you are not madly in love with our hero?'

A strong arm encircled Erin's waist from the other side, sparing her the need to answer. 'Daniel, this is Erin Cassidy,' Tony said. 'I can see that Erin has already guessed our relationship.'

Daniel wrinkled up his brow in a thoughtful frown. 'Erin Cassidy. Erin Cassidy. Where have I heard that name before? Why, you're Allie's disaster,' he guessed in delight. 'She told me all about that tragedy of her young life.' Stepping back, his eyes surveyed Erin from head to toe. 'She said you were nice, but she neglected to mention how beautiful you were.' He shot a keen look at his brother. 'She also neglected to tell me that you and Tony were friendly.'

'We're not, little brother. Erin and I have agreed that we're oil and water, and you know how those mix.'

'Then why are you here together?' Daniel asked.

Tony shrugged. 'It's too long a story to go into now.'

'Meaning, it's none of my business,' Daniel said shrewdly. 'Well, never mind. Let me introduce Erin around. She'll add a little spice to this dull faculty party.'

'Faculty?' Erin asked in surprise.

'Sure. I teach English here at the university. What did Tony tell you I did?'

Erin glared at Tony. 'He let me think you were a football coach.'

'No way. Never mind that I was twice the player he is, I prefer to grovel for pennies instead of having beautiful women fall at my feet.' His huge grin told Erin he was teasing, before he swept her away to meet the other guests.

A couple of hours later, her head ringing with introductions, Erin was happy to escape to the peace of the empty kitchen when Joanna asked for her help.

'I don't really need any help,' Joanna admitted. 'I just wanted to get you alone so I could start the inquisition.'

'Tony and I are just, er, business acquaintances,' Erin said hastily.

Joanna laughed. 'I guess I am pretty obvious. It's just that Tony has never brought a date to any of our parties before, so I was sure that there was something interesting going on.'

'Sorry to disappoint you.'

'I'm not sure you have,' Joanna said cryptically. 'Here, carry this out to the dining-room table, will you?' She handed Erin a large bowl of potato crisps.

There was a buzz of conversation going on around the table, and Erin was quickly welcomed into the group.

Midnight had come and gone when Erin finally said goodbye to Daniel and Joanna. Deep in the canyon, darkness was complete, but the lights were still streaming from the windows of a few isolated homes spotted up and down the hillsides lending a friendly air to the night. Erin settled back against the chilly leather seats of Tony's sports car and kicked off high heels to wriggle her tired feet. Joanna had detained Tony on the porch and Erin could see the other woman clinging to his arm. Tony was vigorously shaking his head in disagreement. He turned and made his way swiftly down to the car. Joanna's pealing laughter followed him.

'Enjoy yourself?' Tony asked shortly as he slammed down on the clutch and jerked the gear lever into place.

'Yes,' Erin answered, surreptitiously tightening her seat-belt as Tony pressed on the accelerator, sending the low-slung car screaming around the canyon curves. Whatever Joanna had said, it must have upset Tony. She added cautiously, 'Daniel and Joanna are really nice. I enjoyed meeting them.'

'Then you weren't bored to death by football talk,' he said in biting tones.

Erin frowned in his direction. Something was definitely bugging him. 'That was mean of you,' she said lightly. 'You might have told me that Daniel was an English instructor at CU.'

'And spoil your anticipation?' he asked coolly.

'You like putting me in the wrong, don't you?'

'Did you think that was your sole prerogative?' he asked savagely.

'I don't know what you mean.'

'Are you trying to sit there and tell me that since we've met, you haven't devoted yourself to putting me in the wrong at every possible opportunity?'

'I've had a lot of help from you to do it,' Erin snapped. Whatever was riling Tony, apparently he needed a scapegoat, and she was elected. She turned to look out of the window with eyes blurred by unshed tears. Tony had been such fun this evening that she had almost forgotten his early words to Daniel. Oil and water, he had called the two of them. She wondered why he had asked her to the party.

'A good question,' he said tersely, when she asked. 'It was pretty obvious that your mother was hinting around that I take pity on her poor, lonely daughter.'

'She was not!' Erin cried angrily.

He ignored her response. 'And, in an odd sort of way, I feel responsible for your break-up with Martin. If he hadn't persuaded himself that we were somehow in competition for your favours, he wouldn't have been so ready to believe the worst of you. I suppose that I shouldn't have spent so much time with your family when I could see that he was misinterpreting my behaviour. He didn't understand that I simply like your family. But how was I to know that your only standards for boyfriends are physical? Any wimp will do. Mental health is obviously not a consideration,' he added caustically.

Erin almost choked on her fury. 'That's unfair,' she cried. 'I had no idea that Martin was the type to have jealous rages. Besides, why should you get so angry?' she went on furiously. 'I'm the one he hit, not you. At least you had the satisfaction of slugging him.'

'Sometimes you say the damnedest things,' he said after a moment. 'Were you going to marry him?'

'Not that it's any of your business, but the subject hadn't come up,' she said stiffly.

'He wasn't your type.'

'Thank you very much for your words of wisdom, but even I can figure out that a man who slaps women isn't my type.' She could sense Tony studying her in the dark, and honesty compelled her to add, 'I don't blame you for what happened. Something would have triggered an outbreak sooner or later. I'm glad that I found out what he was like before things went any further.'

Tony didn't answer, and Erin concentrated on the road before them. A yellow ribbon of light streamed from the steady flow of cars heading west in the opposite lane. Their car topped a small hill, and the lights of Denver spread out before them, the tall downtown skyscrapers rising abruptly out of the flat plains, the golden dome of the Capitol building aglow in the night.

'I meant that Martin wasn't strong enough for you. You'll walk all over any man who isn't strong enough to keep up his side of any relationship,' Tony said, breaking the long period of silence.

Erin didn't need any of his macho advice. 'No wonder you're such a hit with the ladies,' Erin said in disdain. 'You say the sweetest things.'

Tony laughed harshly. 'When I pursue a woman, I say just what she wants to hear. I thought you preferred honesty.' He pulled into the driveway in front of her shuttered house. Switching off the engine, he turned to Erin, his arm resting on the back of her seat. 'Is that what you want? For me to say sweet things to you?' His hand curled around the back of her neck.

'All I want you to say to me is goodbye,' she choked, her traitorous pulse racing at his touch.

Tony slid nearer to her, one hand holding her head immobile. His other hand cupped her face, his thumb rubbing along her chin line. Nervously Erin licked her top lip. Tony's grasp tightened as he bent his head to hers. She shut her eyes, but blotting out the sight of him only made her other senses more aware. The sound of his breathing, the feel of his breath on her face, his scent filling her nostrils, and finally, the taste of his lips as he captured hers. She wanted to fight him, but her body was oddly boneless as he leisurely explored the corners of her mouth before parting her lips. With a small moan of pleasure Erin surrendered to the delicious sensations which threatened to overwhelm her, kissing Tony back with mounting passion. Tony lifted his head, breaking off the contact between their lips. Reluctantly Erin opened her eyes.

'You're so damn beautiful,' Tony whispered huskily. Both hands cradled her face as he studied it intently.

Erin's eyelids dropped in confusion. This man was an enigma to her. One minute berating her, the next praising her. A kiss, light as a butterfly's wing, settled on her lips, but when she would have responded, Tony pulled away.

'It's too bad you're saving yourself for your husband,' he said smoothly from his side of the car.

Shock brought Erin out of her passion-induced daze. 'What?'

'While I can admire your position, unfortunately, it's not one that works to my benefit. Bedding you, knowing what I know, would be like promising commitment, and I don't make promises I have no intention of keeping. So run into the house, little girl, before I change my mind.'

'You're insufferable!' Erin cried. 'You seem to think that the only thing standing between you and me sleeping together is your reluctance. I might have something to say about it, you know.'

Tony shrugged. 'Honey, if I wanted, I could have you in my bed before you could reel off the names of your brothers.'

'You're the most egotistical, arrogant...' The slamming of Tony's door as he got out of the car drowned out her tirade. Brushing aside the hand he extended, she stepped from the car. He rested his hands on the top of his car, an iron arm on either side of her, imprisoning her against the cold metal of the car and the warm bulk of his body. The porch lights were turned on, illuminating the mockery on his face. She stood stiffly, willing her body neither to flinch nor to soften where it came into contact with his. As clearly as if he had spoken, Erin sensed Tony's daring her to struggle against his embrace. But she knew that any such struggle would be an invitation for him to demonstrate his mastery over her. She refused to play any game where his were the only rules. A small whirlwind blew across the driveway, and Erin shivered in the sudden chill.

Tony immediately stepped away from her out of the pool of light. 'Goodnight, Erin,' he said, his voice remote in the darkness.

Incapable of answering, Erin dashed to the house. Closing the front door behind her, she leaned weakly against the wooden panel. Out in the night the low hum of a car engine sounded, and then the street was quiet.

CHAPTER SIX

FOR the next two weeks, Erin tried to put Tony out of her mind. Not easy when she spent the better part of each day working on his window. After a few attempts to hear about the party and getting only monosyllabic answers, Erin's mother had stopped mentioning Tony.

Erin only wished that her younger brother would show the same forbearance. She could have endured Nicky's constantly bemoaning Tony's absence if it weren't for the fact that Nicky had come up with the reason for it.

Reasons, Erin told herself bitterly, as Nicky read aloud at the breakfast table the latest newspaper account of Tony's social activities.

Pursing his lips in a long wolf whistle, Nicky read the caption under a picture. '"Explorer quarterback Tony Hart and Victoria Stephens, daughter of Explorers owner Gil Stephens, trip the light fantastic at charity gala." Wow. No wonder Tony is too busy to come over here. She's something. Tony must have dumped the redhead he was with in yesterday's paper. Look at this.' He shoved the paper before Erin.

Involuntarily she looked down at the paper. The picture of Tony and a tall, sexy-looking blonde stared back up at her. 'Take this paper out of my face, and pass the butter,' Erin said in irritation.

Her brother ignored her, his face wrinkled in thought. 'I've seen this one before, now that I think of it. In fact, I think Tony has had her out three or four times. It must be tough on Tony having to conduct his, er, affairs in the cold glare of publicity. I've got to admire the way he can take out a different woman almost every night. The other women must know what he's doing. It's always in the paper.'

'They probably can't read.' Erin ground the words out between her teeth.

'Oh boy, listen to you. Jealous that you never got your picture in the paper with Tony?' Nicky teased her.

'I can do without that kind of publicity. What's more, I'm sick and tired of having my breakfast ruined by having to listen to you read, morning after morning, about Tony Hart, a subject I have absolutely no interest in. I want you to promise you won't do it any more. Is that clear?'

Apparently it was, because the next morning, although Nicky was silent at the breakfast table, it soon became clear to Erin that her brother was burning to read her something from the paper. She had no intention of relieving him of his promise.

'Erin, you've got to listen to this,' Nicky finally burst out in desperation. 'According to this article, the police have information that Tony is selling drugs.'

'I don't believe it.' Erin snatched the paper from her brother's hands. The article stated that an undisclosed source had informed them that the police department was investigating Tony Hart for dealing in drugs. Officially the police department was refusing to answer any questions, but the anonymous source had leaked that an informant said that he had witnessed the transaction between the quarterback and an unidentified male. According to the newspaper, Tony had been in for unofficial questioning and he had denied all the allegations. The informant had provided the date of the sale, but the accused had been unable to come up with witnesses as to his whereabouts on the date in question, only stating that he had been at home.

'It can't be true. Not Tony.' Nicky looked pleadingly at Erin.

'Of course it's not true. There must be some mistake,' Erin said stoutly. She didn't believe the charges, but even more than her belief in Tony's innocence, she hated the look of hurt and doubt on her younger brother's face as he re-read the incriminating article.

'Wait a minute,' Nicky said in excitement. 'Look at this date, Erin.'

She looked down to where Nicky's finger was pointing. 'So?'

'Don't you see? That's the night of the blizzard. The night you spent at Tony's house. Did he leave the house while you were there?'

'I don't think so,' Erin said slowly.

'There you are,' her brother said triumphantly. 'You're Tony's witness.'

Erin frowned, deep in thought. 'There's only one problem. He could have left. I mean, I was sleeping upstairs, and he was in the basement. I never would have heard him.'

'Erin, do you mean to say you think Tony did what they say?'

Erin thought over Tony's conversations about drugs. There had been no doubt in her mind about his sincerity. 'No, I don't think he did it, Nicky. All I'm saying is that just because I was there doesn't mean that I can prove that Tony was there, too.'

'I wonder why Tony didn't tell them he wasn't alone.' Nicky's thoughts had taken a different direction. 'He must be protecting your reputation.' He glanced slyly at his sister.

'Nicky! If you're implying that I'm thinking about my own reputation at the expense of Tony's, you're wrong. I just don't think that my being there proves anything one way or the other.'

'Where do you suppose the police got their information?' He scanned the article again. 'An anonymous informer. Shoot. I could call up the police and tell them anything about anybody. That doesn't make it true, but I suppose that they'd have to check it out. Anybody else, and no one would even know about it. I suppose it's big news just because he's Tony Hart.'

Erin's mother joined them in the breakfast-room and read the article under discussion. 'Why, that's terrible,' she gasped. 'Poor Tony. Who would say such a thing about him?'

'Maybe Tony's anti-drug campaign is having a detrimental effect on the pushers. Do you suppose a real pusher made up that lie to destroy Tony's reputation? I mean, if he's suspected of dealing in drugs, who's going to believe anything he says?' Nicky asked.

The curious timing of the supposed offence was gnawing away at Erin. Why pick that particular date? Surely anyone trying to discredit Tony would remember the blizzard. A sinking feeling invaded her stomach, and she excused herself from the table. Dialling Martin's number with shaking fingers, she tried to tell herself that he wouldn't have gone that far.

Martin denied her accusation, with such hurt and resentment that Erin was at last convinced that her suspicions were incorrect. Martin had not placed the information against Tony as an act of revenge.

Carolyn and Nicky were still discussing the news when Erin returned to the table. 'Nicky, you're going to miss the school bus,' Erin pointed out.

The two sitting at the table both hastily glanced at the clock, and Nicky stood up reluctantly. 'I've been bragging to all the guys about knowing Tony. I don't know how I can face them today.'

'Nicky Cassidy! If you're a true friend of Tony's, you'll look them all right in the eyeballs and tell them that the entire article is a lie from start to finish,' Erin said explosively.

'You're right, Erin. A man stands by his friends.' He picked up his book bag. 'You won't ever tell Tony I almost let him down, will you?' he asked anxiously.

Knowing better than to hug her brother, Erin contented herself with a poke at his stomach. 'My lips are sealed,' she promised.

'Thanks.' Nicky started out of the door, but then stuck his head back in. 'Be thinking of some way you can prove Tony was there all night. You don't have to say you slept in separate beds...'

'Nicky, go to school!' Erin screeched.

As the door slammed behind him, Carolyn looked enquiringly over at Erin. 'What in the world is Nicky talking about?'

'The date.' Erin pointed to the line in the paper. 'That's the night of the blizzard when I stayed with Tony.'

'I see. And Nicky thinks you ought to lie to protect Tony.'

'Thanks, Mom.'

'For what?'

'For assuming that if I said I slept with Tony, it would be a lie.'

Carolyn smiled. 'I guess I should know my own daughter. All the same, it is strange that whoever started this chose that particular date. You don't suppose...Martin?'

Erin looked glumly at her mother. 'I've already called him. He said no, and he sounded so distressed at the accusation, well, I believed him.' She looked down at the article again. 'Whoever did this obviously never saw Parker after the blizzard, or they'd have realised how impossible it would have been...' A sudden thought struck her. 'Mom, that's it. The snow,' she said excitedly.

'I agree it would be difficult, dear, but Tony's station wagon might have made it.'

'No, no, not that. I saw Tony's driveway and yard the next day, Mom. There were no tyre tracks or footprints in the snow. In fact, no one in the neighbourhood had been out. Tony couldn't possibly have left the house that night after I fell asleep, without leaving some trace of his comings and goings. According to the paper the day after the blizzard, the snow must have stopped shortly after I went to bed, and between then and the next morning no one, but no one, went in or out of Tony's house. I can swear to that.'

'Call your father at work, dear,' said Mrs Cassidy placidly. 'He'll want to go to the police station with you.'

The trip to the police station wasn't as terrible an ordeal as Erin feared. The boxy grey modern building was intimidating, but the detective that she and her father were steered to was polite and professional.

The headlines the next morning attested to her success. *Tony Hart Smeared by Teammate*, read the bold black lettering across the top of the sports page.

'Can you believe this?' Nicky asked in disgust. 'Evan Chase, the third-string quarterback, dreamed up the whole thing. He was hoping to get Tony fired, thought he had a chance to win the starting position from the second-string quarterback. He picked the date of the blizzard because he knew Neal Roberts was out of town and he figured that no one else would have seen Tony then so he wouldn't have any witness to prove his innocence. Chase said he didn't think they would be able to prove anything against Tony, but he hoped if he smeared enough mud on him, some of it would stick.'

'How did the police find out all that so soon?' Erin wanted to know.

'According to the paper, the police were sceptical all along, but then, oops, here you come, Erin. An undisclosed witness provided Tony with an alibi, so they started digging deeper. They didn't even suspect this Chase guy, but he got nervous and spilled the beans.'

'Say what you will about Tony, he is sincere in his anti-drug efforts, and I hated to see his work there sabotaged. I'm just glad it's all over, and quickly,' Erin said in satisfaction.

'Not quite over,' Carolyn said apologetically, looking up from the section of the morning paper that she was reading.

'What do you mean?' Erin asked, startled.

' ''Who is the dark-haired beauty who owned up to sharing Tony Hart's bed, thus providing an alibi for him and dynamiting the drug charges against him?"' Carolyn read.

'Oh, no,' Erin moaned, slumping against her chair. 'The lieutenant promised me total anonymity.'

Her mother quickly searched the article before her. 'Another undisclosed source. I guess if they couldn't get one spicy bit of gossip about Tony, they were pleased to get another.'

'Does it say any more about me?' Erin asked fearfully.

'Hmmm. They describe you pretty well, but at least your name isn't given.'

The newspaper the next morning went into more detail. The reporter had interviewed as many of Tony's recent companions as she could find. Most denied they were Tony's alibi, but several had refused to answer, with such coyness that the reporter had concluded that each wanted the reporter to believe that she was Tony's sleep-in friend. The only problem was, one was a redhead, while the other two were blondes. The reporter went on to say that Tony Hart had disappeared from the social scene the past month, only to return the last two weeks with a vengeance. Was there a broken love affair here? Had Tony's lost love surfaced only to save her former lover? Erin threw the paper across the table. 'I've never read such trash. Who's going to believe all that junk?'

'Apparently a lot of people,' Tony said tightly from the kitchen doorway.

Nicky took one look at Tony's furious face and hastily stood up, disposing of his toast in two enormous bites. 'Gotta run or I'll miss my bus.' He tore out of the door.

Tony stood there, swatting a rolled-up newspaper against his thigh. He didn't say a word, just
glared at Erin.

Finally she could stand the silence no more. 'If
you've come to say thank you, it isn't necessary,'
she said more calmly than she felt. 'I'd have done
the same thing for anyone.'

'Would you really?' Tony sneered. 'Are you sure
that you don't save your heroic gestures for
someone rich and famous?'

Erin gasped. 'What's that supposed to mean?'
The phone rang before Tony could answer, and Erin
rushed to answer it, thankful for the respite.

An unfamiliar female voice asked if she were Erin
Cassidy. When Erin agreed that she was, the voice
asked, 'Is it true that you are Tony Hart's lady-
friend, that you are his mysterious alibi?'

Erin stared at the phone in horror, dragging her
eyes slowly up to meet Tony's as he stood beside
her, having followed her out into the hall. He gave
her a mocking look as the phone squawked in her
hands.

'Who... who is... is that?' she finally managed
to stammer.

The woman identified herself as a reporter for a
local TV channel. 'We'd like to come out and interview you.'

'No, no.' Erin shook her head even as she
mouthed the words.

Tony lifted the phone from her shaking hands
and returned it to its cradle. 'See what you started?'

'How... how did they know? The police
promised...'

'Very convincing, very innocent,' Tony said with
ominous silkiness. 'One would almost think that

you didn't know who was the very busy person calling all the reporters in town yesterday.'

Erin's eyes rounded in horror. 'You think I told them?'

'Not personally. The reporter who got me out of bed this morning assured me that her source was confidential, but also that it was male. Nicky, on the other hand, would do about anything for you, no matter how much he disliked it.'

Erin stared at him in angry disbelief. 'You're crazy,' she finally said. 'Why would I want the whole city talking about me?'

'To force my hand,' Tony answered flatly.

'To do what?' Erin asked, feeling as if she was trapped in a bad dream.

'I've told you often enough that seducing innocent girls carries a responsibility with it. Maybe you thought that I'd feel obliged to make an honest woman out of you.'

Erin was so enraged she could barely spit out the words. 'Do...do you mean...are you saying...dare to stand there...accuse me...I wouldn't marry you...you stupid, arrogant...the last man...' Turning away she dashed angry tears from her eyes.

'You deny going to the police?' Tony's voice was sharp as a whiplash. He grabbed her arm, forcing her to face him.

'Of course not. It's what any decent person would have done. I should have known that you'd misinterpret my actions. I'm sorry I went.' She swallowed the sob in her throat. 'I should have let the lies stand.'

Tony gave her a strange look. 'How did you know the story was a lie? I could have sneaked out without you knowing it.'

'I know you could have, but I also know that
you wouldn't have done what it said. We all knew
it here, in fact, at first Nicky wanted me to...' She
stopped in confusion.

'Nicky wanted you to...' Tony prodded.

Erin could feel warm colour stealing up her face.
'He thought I should tell the police that we, we
were, you know, in the same bed,' she finished with
a rush.

'And did you?'

'No. I didn't have to. Don't you remember? The
next morning when we were shovelling, all that
snow. There wasn't any way you could have gone
out without leaving tracks.'

'I wondered why the police were so sure,' Tony
said thoughtfully. 'Would you have taken Nicky's
advice?'

'Not for you,' Erin snapped. 'For Nicky, and the
other kids like him who believe in you, I might have
thought about it.'

The phone rang before she could say any more.
Tony reached across her and picked it up. A faint
voice asked for Erin Cassidy.

'Wrong number,' Tony snarled before slamming
the phone down. Before it could ring again, he took
it off the hook. The receiver lay on its side, buzzing
like an angry fly.

No angrier than Erin. She followed Tony as he
stalked back out to the kitchen and poured himself
a cup of coffee. He seemed to forget that Erin was
in the room as he paced back and forth across the
floor, scowling ominously. Ignoring him, Erin sat
down in front of her breakfast, pushing the cold
eggs around on her plate. The charged silence of
the room finally prodded her into speech. 'What
right do you have to be so angry?' she asked fu-

riously. 'You've been cleared. I'm the one whose good name is being impugned.'

'You think I don't know that? How do I go about explaining to your parents that in exchange for their friendship I'm responsible for getting their precious daughter's name smeared in the daily news?'

The phone rang, cutting off any answer Erin might have made. They looked at each other in disbelief. The phone couldn't be ringing. Tony had taken it off the hook.

'Erin. Telephone.' Her mother called from the hallway.

'She's not here,' Tony yelled.

'I can't refuse all calls,' Erin protested. 'What if it's business?'

'It's not,' he said, scowling across the room at her.

Carolyn appeared in the kitchen door, a perplexed frown on her face. 'That was some newspaper reporter for you, Erin. I thought Tony said you weren't here.' She looked from one to the other. 'What's wrong? Why was the receiver off the hook?'

'Someone was busy on the phone last night to about every reporter in town identifying Erin as my alibi,' Tony explained tightly.

'Oh, no,' Carolyn said, as she sank down on a kitchen chair, a look of dismay on her face. 'Oh, honey, your father and I shouldn't have let you go. I didn't even think about something like this happening.'

'And let Tony be convicted in the press?' Erin asked.

Carolyn looked guiltily at Tony. 'No, you're right. Forgive me, Tony. I wasn't thinking. I'm so upset.' She waved her hands vaguely in the air. 'I don't understand who would want to do this to Erin.'

Instant understanding flashed into Erin's mind. 'Martin,' she breathed.

'Where would he get the idea of doing something like that?' Tony questioned.

Erin flinched. 'From me,' she confessed. 'When I first read that an anonymous phone caller had alerted the police to your supposed drug dealings, I called up Martin and accused him of doing it. He was very upset, and this is probably his idea of justified revenge. He was just saying what he believed is true.'

'You're defending him?' Tony asked in icy disbelief.

'No, of course not. It was a petty, ugly thing for him to do. He must hate me very much.'

'I should have broken his nose when I had the chance,' Tony said angrily.

'I know how you feel, but that won't solve anything,' Carolyn said. 'We need to stop getting carried away emotionally and think this thing through rationally. My first concern is to see that Erin isn't hurt too badly by it.'

Erin grasped her mother's hand on the table. 'I'll be OK. In a couple of days, something else will wipe it off the front pages, and no one will ever remember anything about it.'

'You're probably right. Why don't you go out of town for a week or so? Visit your friends down in Phoenix or go and stay with your Aunt Gerry in Miami. She'd love to have you.'

'I really don't think that's necessary. I'll just write up a written statement or something telling the truth and pass it out to reporters,' Erin suggested.

'Do you really think they'll believe you?' Carolyn asked.

'Why not?'

'Because of me, that's why not,' Tony said heavily. 'How could you forget my reputation that you're constantly throwing in my face? Not one reader out of a hundred is going to believe that a beautiful girl like you spent the night at my house sleeping all alone in my bed.'

There was no denying the truth of Tony's words. Erin and her mother stared speechlessly at each other, Carolyn's face full of chagrin.

'Don't look like that, Carolyn.' Tony stepped up behind Erin's mother and gripped her shoulder hard. 'I have an idea. Erin won't like it, but it's the best I can think of to make amends.'

'Tony, this wasn't your fault,' Carolyn assured him, but Erin could see the hope on her mother's face. Somewhere deep inside Erin a cold chill invaded her bones as she waited in bleak anticipation of Tony's idea.

'We could do a little leaking of our own. Let the word slip that Erin and I are unofficially engaged.'

'No!'

Tony ignored Erin's swift denial. 'I've got a reporter friend or two who owe me some favours. I can tip them off who to ask to find out that Erin and I met at Merry's party, to check with your neighbours who will agree that my car is here frequently. My brother could admit that I brought Erin to his house to introduce her to my family. We won't make any announcements that might make it look like this is something ginned up to save Erin's reputation, but a few leaks and hints and everyone will get the idea.'

'It might work.' Carolyn wrinkled her brow thoughtfully.

'I won't do it,' Erin said firmly. 'I will not pretend to be engaged to Tony.'

'I think the best thing,' Tony went on as if Erin hadn't spoken, 'is for all involved to insist that we are just good friends. That will really convince everyone that we are much more.'

'Aren't you forgetting something?' Erin asked with false sweetness. 'Like the fact that for the past two weeks you've been photographed with a different woman almost every night, and none of those women has been me. Who's going to believe that all this time you were supposedly going with me?' Knowing she had presented him with an insurmountable obstacle, Erin smirked in triumph.

Tony grinned wickedly back. 'Ah, but the newspaper has already explained that. We had a lovers' quarrel. I was obviously dating all those women to make you jealous. Nothing worked, until you woke up one morning and read about my troubles. Loyal and loving as you are, you immediately let bygones be bygones and rushed to my rescue.'

'That's disgusting,' Erin said.

'No, that's love.' Tony sighed gustily, a hand held to his heart.

Erin was not amused. 'If I was your lover, why didn't you tell the police that in the beginning and have an alibi?'

'A gentleman never tells,' he pointed out with a martyred air.

'Anyway, your stupid solution would be the same as if I came right out and admitted that I was sleeping with you,' Erin objected.

'In the first place, you can deny that you were in my bed until the cows come home, and no one is going to believe you. In the second place, I'm not advocating that you go around and announce to the world that we are lovers, merely that by letting people think that we are practically engaged, it takes the edge off the titillating aspect of the situation. These days no one thinks anything about a man and woman jumping the gun a little.'

'I do,' Erin said stormily. 'And I think your idea stinks and I'm not going to do it. Anyone asks, and I'll tell them exactly what happened.'

Tony shrugged. 'Your funeral.'

'Erin, please don't be hasty.' Carolyn spoke up in her soft voice. 'Tony's idea does have some merit. I hate to have you the object of such unpleasant speculation.'

Erin turned to her mother, and was immediately smitten by the drawn look on her mother's face. All this dissension and turmoil could not be good for a woman recovering from a stroke. If Tony were correct and no one believed Erin's story, her mother would suffer even more from her daughter's notoriety. She thought of her brothers and her father and how protective of her they were. She thought of Nicky's reluctance to face his friends at school after the allegations against Tony were printed in the paper. How much worse it would be for him to have to defend his sister's honour. And defend it he would, if it meant a fist fight every day and losing every friend he had. Could Erin put her family through all that, and in the end, convince no one of her innocence? Who was going to believe that any woman could turn down handsome, charming, rich Tony Hart, a man considered to be a Don Juan without peer when it came to feminine conquests?

'All right,' she reluctantly capitulated. 'I'll go along with Tony's plan, but I don't like it.'

'You think I do?' Tony asked savagely. 'The last thing I want is to be saddled with a Victorian fiancée.'

Carolyn stood up. 'I'll leave you two to sort out the details. You can count on the family to back you up.'

'I know that.' Tony pressed a warm kiss on Carolyn's brow. 'Thanks for not hating me for this.'

'You can't be blamed for the behaviour of two people who were so blinded by jealousy that they failed to see how many others were going to be hurt by their actions. I know how unpleasant this is for you both.'

Erin stared at her plate as her mother left the room, feelings of bitterness welling up inside her. What had she ever done to Martin to deserve this? As for that other creep, the football player, she didn't even know who he was, yet his net of intrigue had managed to entangle and drag her down.

'Thinking of new invectives to use against me?' Tony asked abruptly, leaning against the counter watching her.

'No,' Erin said wearily. 'I'm just wondering why. And how. You go through life thinking you are making your own choices and then something like this happens out of the blue and you realise how helpless you are, how at the mercy of complete strangers a person can be.'

'You could have stayed home that day. Heaven knows, the radio issued enough weather bulletins. Anyone with half a brain would have listened.'

'You're blaming me for this whole mess?' Erin cried. 'That's unfair. If I had stayed home that day, who would have come forth and alibied you?'

'For your information, despite your opinion of me, the police never believed that I was dealing drugs.'

'You know I never believed that you were. But the paper...'

'The paper was tipped off by Chase. When the information he'd given anonymously to the police didn't leak out to the press as he'd hoped, he got on the phone himself. Naturally, when reporters started snooping around, the police couldn't deny that the charges had been made. Despite their personal opinions, they had to investigate the allegations, but I sure didn't need Joan of Arc rushing to my rescue. The whole mess would have been cleared up in a few weeks.'

'By which time half the state would have decided that there must be some truth to the story,' Erin retorted. 'I should have known better than to expect thanks from you.'

'Considering to what lengths I went to to keep your name out of it, I should think so,' Tony answered furiously. 'At least I had enough sense to look ahead and see the possibility of this happening.'

'The police promised me total anonymity. How could I know that Martin would blabber everything to the world?'

'He was your friend,' Tony said nastily. 'I'm not the one who dated him for months without a clue to his real personality.'

'Get out!' Erin choked, on the verge of tears. 'I've had about all of you I can take today.'

'Fine. I will, but I'll be back. We're in love, remember?' he asked sarcastically. He yanked her chair away from the table, and grabbing her arm, pulled her to her feet. 'Walk me to the door.'

'No.' She tried to twist out of his grasp, but his hand was locked on her arm, forcing her down the hall with him.

Outside on the front porch, Tony pulled her into his arms.

'No,' Erin breathed in protest.

'Don't fight me,' he said from between gritted teeth as his face lowered to hers.

Erin closed her eyes, but his angry face was imprinted on her brain. An iron band around her waist held her tightly against his chest and she wondered if the pounding of her heart was as obvious to him as it was to her. The smell of roses drifted by on the morning breeze to be overridden by the scent of aftershave and coffee as Tony lowered his mouth to hers. The frantic barking of a large dog in the park was answered by the indignant honking of the Canada geese. Nearer to her, the sound of Tony's breathing mingled with her own. She didn't know what she expected, but Tony's lips were warm against hers, a light pressure that lasted mere seconds. He made no attempt to deepen the kiss but raised his head almost immediately. Erin blinked up at him in confusion.

He dropped a light kiss on her forehead. 'Smile at me,' he ordered.

'I won't,' she said mutinously.

'Damn it, Erin, do you ever do what you're told?' The exasperated words made a mockery of the smile painted on his face. 'There's a newspaper reporter camped out across the street. No, don't look,' he ordered as she made an involuntary movement. 'He's been there at least since I arrived, but I pretended that I didn't see him. If you won't smile.' He turned so that her back was to the street.

'You ba...'

Tony shut her up, pressing his mouth to hers in a punishing kiss. No doubt to their audience it seemed passionate, Erin thought in disgust. Silently she fought him, refusing to part her lips, refusing to yield to his superior strength. He backed off with a harsh laugh. 'I just wish my offensive line could block as well as you do,' he said. To her growing fury, he patted her behind and then shoved her through the door into the house. Only the thought of the unwelcome audience kept her from throwing open the door and beaning him with one of the flower-pots that stood on the porch. She could hear his footsteps descending the porch stairs. From across the street a voice hailed him. Tony's steps hesitated, and then he answered the voice.

Tony returned before dinner. Erin answered the door when he arrived. Closing the door behind him, he dipped his head and kissed her swiftly on the lips.

She jerked her head back. 'Don't tell me we have hidden TV cameras in our hall,' she asked coldly.

Tony's lips twitched as if he were hiding a grin. 'You had such a look of dreaded anticipation on your face, I didn't want to let you down.'

Erin's eyes narrowed. Tony's hostility of the morning had apparently evaporated. Had he thought over the situation and decided he could use it to his advantage? She would soon disabuse him of that notion. 'If you think this stupid, mock engagement is licence for you to grab me every time you get the urge, you've got another think coming.'

Just then Nicky erupted from the living-room. 'Tony, you're just the guy I want to see. Tell Erin that it's stupid for her to drag me down to some art museum next week just because she wants company.'

'I told you, Nicky,' Erin said heatedly. 'I don't need company. I just think it's time you realised there is more to life than football.'

'I already know that,' Nicky insisted. 'There's basketball, baseball, soccer, track...' He grinned wickedly at his sister.

'That's not what I mean, and you know it.' Erin glared back at her brother.

'I'll bet Tony doesn't waste his time in art museums,' Nicky declared huffily.

'You're right. I don't waste my time in art museums.'

'Thanks, Tony,' Erin turned on him in disgust. 'I might have known you'd agree with him.'

'Whoa. I said I didn't waste my time. I don't consider time spent in art museums as a waste of time.' Sister and brother both stared at him in astonishment. His eyes flashed with amusement as he looked at Nicky. 'In fact, I'll go with Erin, too.'

'Good. If you're going with her, I won't need to go,' Nicky said.

'Nicky!' Erin screeched, but before she could further remonstrate with her brother, Tony spoke up.

'No, I don't know that you need to go. I have to admit I'm disappointed. I thought you were——oh well, never mind.'

'What do you mean?' Nicky asked suspiciously.

Tony shrugged. 'A man never stops learning. He absorbs all the knowledge that he possibly can, because he never knows when it will come in handy.'

'I don't see where seeing some stupid old pictures is ever going to do anything for me,' Nicky said stubbornly.

'Let me give you an example,' Tony drawled. Laughter lurked in the corners of his eyes as his gaze lingered on Erin's face. 'Erin has a face that Botticelli would have been crazy to paint, and if I told her that, she'd be putty in my hands.'

'Hardly,' Erin hotly contradicted him, at the same time feeling a warm glow of pleasure.

He ignored her interruption. 'However, if I told her that she'd be a perfect model for Rubens, she'd probably throw something at me since his models were usually a little on the robust side, which Erin is definitely not.' Erin stared at him in disbelief. Whoever heard of a football player who knew that a Rubens wasn't a sandwich?

Tony encircled her waist with his arm, grinning down at her. 'Unless you're trying to catch flies, shut your mouth.' Erin's pulse speeded up as Tony's gaze captured hers.

'Sicko,' Nicky said in disgust. 'If you guys are going to stand here in the hall and make goo-goo eyes at each other, I'm going back in to watch the basketball game on TV. You coming, Tony?'

'In a minute.' Tony looked expectantly at Erin. 'Well, don't I deserve thanks?'

'For what?'

'Talking Nicky into going to the museum with us.'

'I didn't hear him say he was going.' The significance of what he had said hit her. 'What do you mean, us?'

'After that big spiel to Nicky, would I dare not go?'

'And you didn't mean a word of it, did you?' Erin swallowed her disappointment. He had probably read the line about Rubens and Botticelli in some men's magazine and used it all the time.

'Tony, quick! Come see this instant replay. It's great.' Doyle's voice came from the living-room.

Erin started to move away. Tony's arm tightened about her waist. 'No, you don't. If you expect Nicky to go to the art museum with you, you can come watch the game with him.'

CHAPTER SEVEN

DOYLE and Nicky looked up in surprise as Erin walked in and sat down on the sofa beside Tony, but they made no comment about her presence, quickly drawing Tony into their discussion about the game. Erin's attention soon wandered from the action on the screen.

Tony poked her. 'He writes poetry,' he said, pointing to the man running down the court with the ball. The player scored, and the three men in the living-room cheered. Erin wriggled restlessly on the sofa, overcome by boredom. What a tedious way to spend an evening.

An advertisement flashed on the screen, and Nicky and his dad took the opportunity to head for the kitchen. 'It's not so bad, is it?' Tony asked Erin.

'No,' she lied politely.

Tony chuckled. 'I can tell you're not impressed. That's because you don't know what's going on.'

'Sure I do. The guys in green are trying to put the ball into that basket thing more often than the guys in white can do it.'

'Well, I have to admit you have the basics there,' Tony teased her. The game came back on. 'Watch that guy with the ball. As fast as he's moving, he knows where every one of his team mates is. Look at that.' The player tossed the ball over his shoulder, seemingly without looking, to another player on his team. 'That guy is thinking, always thinking. He's studied, he's practised, he's honed his skills, and now all that comes together with hard work and dedication.'

'To win a game,' Erin pointed out.

'Right. To win a game. And give entertainment to a lot of people like your dad and Nicky. And me. Do you like movies?'

'Some,' she answered cautiously. 'Why?'

'And why do you go? To be entertained,' he answered his own question. 'It's the same with watching professional sports. Maybe things aren't going so well in your life, but for the length of a movie, or a game, you can escape into someone else's world and forget your own. Maybe you goofed up at work and the boss dumped on you, so you're feeling pretty low, like a loser. Now suppose you identify with some particular team and that team wins a big ballgame. You feel good, at least for a little while.'

'Reality is still there when the game is over,' Erin said drily.

'I'm not denying that. But maybe by distancing yourself from your problems for a short while, you can gain a new perspective on them and find a way to deal with them. Besides, rooting for the home team is like belonging to a club. It fosters a sense of community between people of diverse backgrounds and interests.'

'That's attributing pretty lofty benefits to a sport like football where the sole aim seems to be to crunch each other on the field.'

'The goal isn't crunching, the goal is winning,' Tony said. 'Your problem is that you're condemning something you know absolutely nothing about.'

'That's not my problem,' Erin countered sweetly. 'I couldn't care less what the aim of the game is.

Your problem is in persisting in thinking that I have a problem just because I don't happen to agree with you.' She got up to leave.

Just then Nicky and her dad returned with plates of sandwiches and drinks. 'Quitter,' Tony said quietly in her ear.

Erin dropped back on to the sofa. She would sit through this entire game even if it killed her, and it just might. At least then they couldn't accuse her of not giving it a chance.

Nicky was talking to Tony. 'Didn't you say once that you knew him?' he asked, pointing to one of the players.

'Sure. Now there's a man with enough energy for ten people. He's devoted to programmes dealing with special children, those with mental and physical disabilities, and he works tirelessly getting other sports figures involved. He refuses to take a dime for his work with the various organisations and foundations. Says he's just giving back a little of his own good fortune.'

Then the three men were caught up in the excitement of the game, and the conversation dealt solely with things like rebounds, defence and field goals. Erin let her mind wander. She was well aware that much of Tony's conversation was designed to illustrate to her that the players were individuals and that she shouldn't try to fit them all into some preconceived role and judge them accordingly. It was certainly true that Tony resisted all her efforts to think of him as just a dumb jock. She thought of her own brothers. While it was true that sports were a major part of all their lives, maybe they weren't as one-dimensional as she had always thought. There was Kevin, who struggled to put his thoughts and feelings on paper. Years of football hadn't doused his creative spirit. And Baird, who played college football on Saturdays and played the drums on Sunday with a small group of rock-music-loving friends. Even Alan, who coached, and Rourke, the ex-college-star, probably had other interests that she had never bothered to dig out. She had always condemned them for their lack of interest and support for her activities. Could it be that they felt the same about her? Her attention was drawn to Nicky. His face was alight with excitement as he discussed the game with their father and Tony. By refusing to share their interests, had she somehow put up fences between herself and her brothers? Fences had gates, she told herself stoutly.

She concentrated on the game, trying to overlook dripping sweat, bodies colliding with each other and the floor, mouthpieces that made disgusting appearances, and men who had a tendency to spit into paper cups just when the camera caught them close-up. Cautiously at first, and then with greater interest when Nicky didn't ridicule her, she began quizzing the men about the aspects of the game which puzzled her.

Erin was relieved when the basketball game finally ended. She wouldn't go so far as to say she had become an instant fan, but at least, with a little coaching, she had gained a few insights about the game. As Nicky and her father left the room to get ready for dinner, she looked expectantly at Tony.

He stood up. 'I'll go and thank your mom for the sandwiches, and then I'm off,' he said brusquely. He left the room, leaving a surprised and somewhat disappointed Erin sitting on the sofa. What did you expect? she chided herself. Praise, because she was a good girl and did what Tony told her to do? Obviously he was so accustomed to people bedazzled by his money and talent that he didn't find it necessary to develop little quirks of personality like kindness, decency, and politeness. She could count herself lucky that her engagement to him was only make-believe. His rapid switches in mood left her feeling totally confused. One minute he was smiling and friendly, the next snarling at her like an escaped tiger from the zoo. Snarling, perhaps, whenever he remembered that he had to pretend to be engaged to her.

She was still brooding over Tony's ping-pong behaviour the next evening as she ran lightly down the staircase in her home. Half-way down she stopped abruptly, staring at her father standing in the front hallway below.

He looked up. 'What's the matter? Don't you like my tie?' he asked self-consciously.

Erin moved slowly down the steps. 'The tie is fine. I was just wondering why you are all spiffed up.'

Doyle stood in front of the mirror, tugging at the knot under his chin. 'Darn tie,' he muttered. 'Never can get them straight.'

'You didn't say where you were going,' Erin reminded him as she stood in front of him and adjusted the tie.

He looked over her bent head into the mirror. 'To a concert with your mom,' he said casually.

Erin looked at him in astonishment. 'You're kidding.'

'Why should I be kidding?' he asked in a peeved tone of voice. 'Carrie was going with her friend Ellen, but Ellen's daughter is sick, so Ellen had to cancel. Couldn't see your mother going alone. The tickets cost too much for her to just throw them away.'

'I can't believe that you are actually taking Mom to a concert.'

'I don't know why you're making a federal case out of it.'

'You have to admit, it's not your usual behaviour.'

'There's a certain truth in what you say,' Doyle admitted. 'It's a funny thing. I've been married to your mother for thirty-two years, and I thought I knew all there was to know about her. I knew when I met her that Carrie liked movies, exhibits, museums and all that cultural stuff. When we first got married I offered to go along with her a couple of times, but she always told me to go to a football game or something, so I just gave up asking. I thought she didn't want me along, that she figured I'd ruin her time since I didn't know anything about that stuff. How was I supposed to know that she thought that I didn't really want to go, that I was merely asking to be polite? Hell's bells, maybe I didn't know much about that highfalutin' stuff, but just being with Carrie would have made it interesting. She tried to convince me she didn't want me to go tonight, but I insisted. I should have insisted years ago.'

'What made you insist this time?' Erin asked out of curiosity.

'Something your mom said when she was talking to Tony. She wasn't complaining, mind you, but I got the idea that she agreed with him when he said that married couples should share some interests.'

'Tony said that?'

Her father nodded his head. 'When you and Tony get married, Erin, never assume you know how the other person feels. Ask. And don't answer by saying what you think Tony wants to hear. For thirty-two years your mom and I went our own way, each thinking we were doing what the other one wanted, when all along, maybe what we wanted was to do things together. *Thirty-two years.* Not exactly wasted years, but years that might have been better, richer, if we'd just been honest with what we wanted out of this marriage. I might have lost Carrie when she had her stroke. God was good enough to give us a second chance, and this time, we mean to do it right. I just hope it's not too late to teach an old dog new tricks.'

'Of course it's not,' Erin said huskily, as she rubbed her cheek affectionately against her father's shoulder. Now didn't seem to be the right time to remind him that she and Tony weren't getting married. Especially when she looked up the stairs and saw her mother coming down. There was a look of expectancy on her mother's face that rivalled that of any young girl going to her first prom. Erin tried to swallow the huge lump that suddenly appeared in her throat. She had never realised how beautiful her mother was.

Doyle echoed her thoughts. 'It's a good thing Tony's not here. He wanted to marry you when he tasted your apple pie.' He noisily cleared his throat. 'He'd probably consider making you a widow if he saw you in that dress. New, isn't it?'

Well aware that her mother had been wearing the dress to concerts for at least the past five years, Erin looked to her mother to share her amusement at her father's comment, but Carolyn just blushed and handed her wrap to Doyle. Feeling an unwelcome third, Erin slipped into the living-room.

Her mother's obvious pleasure about the evening and her father's comments gave Erin much to ponder over. Thirty-two years, her dad had said.

Thirty-two years of a seemingly happy and content life. Erin tried to deny the suffocating guilt that threatened to engulf her. She had never even considered that there might be hidden dissatisfactions. How could that be? Had she and her brothers been so blindly pursuing their own interests that they had been unable to see what lay right before their eyes? Why did it have to be Tony who had dug beneath the surface and prised out all their family secrets? Who did he think he was? Some tin god who reached down and stirred up other people's lives with his little finger?

'How was the concert, Mom?' Erin asked the next morning at breakfast, still overcome with shame to think that she had blithely dismissed her mother's happiness.

'It was wonderful.' Carolyn laughed quietly. 'Your father didn't even fall asleep. Afterwards we went out for coffee and a snack. Incidentally, your father and I won't be home for dinner tonight. We thought we'd just grab a bite at the game.'

'Game?'

'There's some kind of basketball play-off at McNichols Sports Arena, and your dad asked me to go with him.'

'And you're going?' Erin asked in astonishment. 'I thought you hated sports.'

Carolyn grimaced. 'I know. But your dad convinced me that it might be kind of fun.' She paused. 'Just between you and me, Erin, I think that Doyle has suddenly realised that in a few more years, Nicky will be away at college, and he won't have any of his boys left to go places with him.' She giggled like a young girl. 'I guess you could say I'm in training.'

'You don't mind?' Erin gave her mother an anxious look.

Her mother coloured softly. 'No, I don't mind. I think a couple goes through several stages in life. The honeymoon stage, the raising a family stage, and then the stage your father and I are about to begin. With you and Rourke both married and all the other boys but Nicky gone and living their own lives, it's time for your father and me to start new lives of our own. I've been so busy with you children...last night is the first time that Doyle and I have talked, really talked, about our dreams and hopes...' She stirred her coffee dreamily. 'Oh dear,' she sat up straight, a guilty look on her face. 'Is Tony planning on coming to dinner tonight? I had thought that you and Nicky could go out for a hamburger or something, but if Tony is coming...'

'I don't know, and if he does, he can eat a hamburger, too,' Erin said firmly. 'You and Dad have a good time tonight.' She doubted if her mother heard her as she left for the studio. The dreamy look was back on her mother's face. Erin didn't even bother to point out to her mother that she wasn't married, or about to be.

Erin didn't need to look out of the door later that morning when she heard the footsteps on the staircase. The tune that Tony was loudly whistling announced his identity. He must have an ancient songbook to come up with all these popular old Irish tunes.

'Knock, knock.' His rugged face appeared in the doorway. 'I just saw Carolyn. She told me that she's going to the basketball game tonight.'

The look of satisfaction on his face rekindled Erin's grievance against him. If he expected her to gush with gratitude just because he had seen, at practically a glance, what she and her brothers had lived with and overlooked all these years, he could just think again. 'Why are you here?' she asked, her voice cool.

'I take it you disapprove of your mother going to the game.'

'I never said that.'

Raising one eyebrow in disbelief, Tony said nothing, but strolled around her workroom, stopping to investigate whatever took his interest. Erin tried to ignore him as she applied oleic acid flux to the edges of the copper foil on the window in front of her, but when he came to stand behind her, she put down her flux brush. 'Did you want something?'

Tony eyed her curiously. 'I can't decide if this is simply your usual unpleasant attitude towards me, or if you've come up with some new sin to add to the account you seem to keep about me.'

Erin picked up a reasonably clean rag and wiped her hands. 'I'm sure a Rhodes scholar like you can find the answer to that,' she said nastily.

Tony whistled between pursed lips. 'Really annoyed. OK. I'll play your guessing game. There aren't any reporters at your door, so you're not irritated about that. You've already thrown your tantrum about the engagement, and I don't think you're one to beat a dead horse.'

'Thanks for the kind words,' she snapped.

'I was right the first time, wasn't I?' he said slowly. 'You're annoyed that your mother is going to the game with your dad tonight, and somehow you've managed to pin the blame for that on me.'

'Why should I be mad about that?'

'Because she's letting your team down, going over to the enemy.'

'That's ridiculous!'

'Is it? You're feeling sorry for yourself because you're worried that if your mom gets interested in sports, she'll lose interest in the kinds of things that you two share now.'

'That's not true,' Erin choked. 'I thought that she was happy. I decided years ago that I'd never marry a man who ignored me for his sports, but I never dreamed that Mom was dissatisfied.' Realisation slowly dawned on Tony's face as she continued to pour out her inner guilt. 'I'm her daughter. I should have known.'

'Don't blame yourself, Erin. Whatever your folks made of their marriage was their decision. It had nothing to do with you. It's their marriage, not yours.'

She dashed hot tears from her eyes before turning furiously to him. 'Who appointed you such an expert on marriage? The last I heard you were an avowed bachelor who thought that the married state was for the birds.'

'Not for the birds, just not for me,' Tony pointed out. He fiddled with the tools on her bench, in such a way that were he anyone else, she'd have said he was nervous.

'Leave my things alone. I don't like people messing with my tools,' she blurted out.

Tony jammed his hands into his pockets. 'Sorry.'

Such a bleak look settled on his face, that Erin rushed to explain. 'It's just that I have this thing about people touching my stuff. It may not look like it, but I'm very organised, and if someone moves a tool, it drives me to distraction.'

'That's OK,' he said, his mind clearly on something else, something unpleasant.

Erin opened the bottle of flux and began brushing it over the copper foil, all the while watching Tony out of the corner of her eye. Something was eating on him. Finally she could stand it no longer, and she tossed her brush on the table. 'What's wrong?' she asked.

'What makes you think something is?' he countered.

'Because the last time I saw that look, Nicky was wearing it when his pet hamster died.'

'Oh.' Seeing that she expected more, he added, 'I was just thinking about what I said to you. That kids aren't responsible for the state of their parents' marriage. I wish that someone had been around about fifteen years ago to drum that into my head.'

Erin tried to remember what she'd read about his parents. She didn't think that they were divorced.

'A kid never thinks much about his folks' love life,' Tony said softly, almost to himself. 'I mean, I guess I figured mine slept together—after all, they had three kids. I never saw them hug or kiss each other, but they never fought much, so everything seemed OK. Then, one night...' He broke off, crossing the room to look out of the window overlooking the park.

'One night I was driving around, the way high-school kids do, and I saw my dad's car parked outside this schoolteacher's house. I couldn't figure out why he was there. She'd been my teacher a few years before, but none of us had her at that time. I thought about it and went around the block again. Finally—and to this day I don't know why I did it, it wasn't like I really thought my dad was doing anything there—wrong, I mean.'

He glanced back at Erin as if asking her to understand why he had done what he had done. At the same time, there was a look of grim foreboding on his face, and she spoke up quickly. 'You don't have to tell me this.'

He nodded, not in agreement, but in acknowledgement of her statement. 'I parked my car a block away and sneaked up to the teacher's house. The curtains were pulled, but they didn't quite meet, and there was a narrow strip that I could see through.' Erin held her breath in uneasy anticipation. She could see the muscles of Tony's neck clenched with tension.

'My dad and this teacher were lying on the couch. I could only see parts of them, but I knew what they were doing.'

Tony grew silent, and Erin could see that he was still struggling with the memory of his painful discoveries. 'I couldn't decide what to do,' he said finally. 'So I started following him. My own dad. Spying on him.'

'It must have been terrible for you.'

'I couldn't tell Mom. I knew how it would hurt her. Daniel and Allie were too young to discuss it with them.' His voice trailed away.

Erin's heart went out to the teenager that Tony had been. To possess such a horrible secret and be unable to share it. Even for his strong shoulders, the burden must have been unbearable.

'I finally went to my dad,' Tony continued, his voice thick with emotion. 'At first he was mad, really mad at me. We yelled a lot at each other, threatened dumb stuff. But I guess he felt guilty, too, and I think that he was relieved to be caught. He couldn't tell me about it fast enough.' He hunched his shoulders as if to ward off the remembered suffering.

'My folks live on a small farm in central Nebraska. They were married young because my mother was pregnant—with me. I guess things were OK at first, but eventually Dad grew restless. He'd wanted to go places, do things, and there he was, tied down to a family. Mom was busy with us kids, and they drifted apart. He swore that he still loved her, that this other thing, with the teacher, just happened.'

Hands still jammed in his pockets, he drew lines in the glass dust on the floor with the toe of his shoe. 'He wanted me to understand, but I didn't. Mom was working so hard, and instead of helping her out, it seemed to me that he was acting like a spoiled child, whining because he wasn't getting enough attention.'

Erin moved silently to Tony's side. If only there were something that she could do or say to ease his pain.

'Dad and I never talked about it again. That summer the teacher moved away. Dad stayed with Mom, and I don't know if he ever told her about his straying or not. I never asked.' He shrugged. 'I've wished a million times that I'd driven on when I saw his car and not spied on him. He's never really forgiven me. We're polite to each other these days, nothing more.' Tony glanced down at Erin. 'That's one of the reasons why I enjoy coming to your house so often. Everyone in your family truly likes everyone else. Sure, you all have separate interests, and there's a lot of clowning around and teasing, but the bottom line is, there's a great deal of love and respect between all of you. It's all you've ever known, so you take it for granted, but believe me, Erin, you have a very special family.'

Erin blinked eyes suddenly moist. 'I do know it, but you're right. Sometimes we forget it.' She hesitated. 'Tony, I'm sorry.'

'Why? Because my dad was the type who should never have got married?' The moment for confidences was gone. His tone forbade her to offer sympathy.

'No, not that,' she said slowly. 'I'm sorry that I was...was mad at you. I felt terrible that I didn't...that you did...'

'In fact, you resented like hell that a dumb athlete like me picked up on something that you, with all your artistic sensitivities, missed.'

The edge of sarcasm to his voice instantly ignited Erin's temper, sweeping away the embryonic feelings of understanding and compassion that she had begun to feel for Tony. 'You never did say what you wanted,' she reminded him coldly.

'I don't suppose you'll believe that I just came by to see your smiling face.'

'No.'

'In that case,' he went on, undaunted by her bald answer, 'I came to find out why my window is taking so long. I have the wood I plan to frame it with, and I'm anxious to get started.'

Erin stiffened at his implied criticism. 'I had some trouble finding all the glass I wanted, not to mention that there's been a certain amount of turmoil in my life lately,' she said defensively. 'I'm trying to work on it now, but with all these distractions...' She paused, her meaning clear.

Tony moved closer to her. 'Are you saying that I'm a distraction?' he asked, his voice soft and sensuous.

Erin felt her heart stop, then start up again at an erratic pace. Tony played this game too well. She willed her voice to remain calm. 'Anyone blundering around my workshop is a distraction.'

Reaching over, he cupped her chin firmly in his large hand, holding her face immobile for his inspection. 'I'm just another customer, in fact,' he suggested. 'No one special.'

'Exactly.' She swallowed convulsively under the hypnotic effect of his blue eyes, darkened by some strange emotion. It was taking all her energy to resist the magnetic pull of his body.

'Liar.' His lips twisted with amusement as he lowered his head to hers. 'That little pulse in your throat is beating like a caged bird, frantic to escape.' The softly muttered words fell like gentle rain against the corner of her mouth. Like the parched desert welcomes the spring rains, she turned her head to meet his lips. Little persuasion was needed to part a mouth eager to taste of the special delights that were his alone to give her. Her arms locked behind his neck, holding his mouth to hers. When he moved, it was only to shift to a more comfortable position, leaning against her work bench, Erin held securely between his thighs.

The familiar scents of her workshop faded away to be replaced by the seductive scent of Tony's skin with its faint traces of soap and aftershave. The heavy fragrance from the climbing roses on the garage wall drifted through the open window and transformed her workshop into a perfumed bower. A house finch nesting beneath the eaves burst into a joyous song, serenading them as well as his mate. Tony's thighs were heated iron bars clamped alongside Erin's jean-clad legs. Her hands crept down his neck to his shoulders and gloried in the powerful muscles that contracted under her stroking fingers. His mouth left hers, trailing feathery-light kisses along her jaw bone. She buried her face in his neck, breathing deeply of his scent, as she sought to control the riotous emotions that ran amok throughout her body. Calloused fingertips trailed their way down her neck and quickly disposed of the barriers between them and her swelling breasts. An electric shock galvanised Erin's body as his enormous palms slowly rubbed her breasts, the rough texture of his skin exquisite torment against the sensitive tips.

Tony's hands stilled at her convulsive movement. 'I keep forgetting how innocent you are,' he muttered. His hands remained cupped warmly around her breasts an eternal second longer while Erin waited for him to resume his sensual teasing of the hardened nubs. Instead, he slowly reclothed her nudity. She shut her eyes to hide her hurt and disappointment from the intense scrutiny she could feel him subjecting her to. 'Sorry, little girl.' There was genuine regret in his voice.

Erin immediately rejected his sympathy. How dare he feel sorry for her! Did he think that she was so besotted with him that she craved his arms and his kisses? Damn his arrogant ego! 'That's OK,' she said coolly, thankful that the quivering of her muscles, still tingling from Tony's erotic touch, was not reflected in her voice. 'As you say, I'm still a beginner at this lovemaking business.'

Something in her tone must have alerted Tony and he looked sharply at her. 'What's that got to do with anything?'

She looked back at him in wide-eyed innocence. 'I've been learning a lot from you, Tony. When it comes to sexual skills, you're the master. Any woman would be thrilled to have you as her tutor in an area this, er, sensitive. At first, I was upset about this engagement business, but then I saw that it would be dumb of me not to take advantage of such a wonderful opportunity.'

'Are you trying to tell me that you consider my kisses a way for you to gain experience?' He spat out the words, his face dark with anger.

Her heart thudded sickeningly at the look of naked fury on his face. She tried calmly to survey her outspread hands to show Tony how little he affected her, but she feared her shaking fingers would betray her, so she clenched them into fists and thrust them deep into her jean pockets. 'Of course. And, the best part is, there's no risk involved. I mean, I know that I can count on you, to, er, well, you know, not go all the way,' she added ingenuously.

'I wouldn't be so sure of that,' Tony ground out savagely.

Erin immediately assumed an air of spurious sympathy and understanding. 'I know,' she nodded sagely. 'It must be terribly difficult for you. I'm awfully sorry about that.'

He stared suspiciously at her. 'I know I'm going to hate myself for asking,' he said bitterly, 'but why difficult for me?'

'You can hardly be engaged to one woman and dating others at the same time,' she pointed out. 'It must be terrible on your sex life. I mean, I know you're not used to all this enforced abstinence.'

Tony was out of the door, his back stiff with murderous rage, and Erin leaned against her work bench, supported by legs that threatened to collapse under her at any minute. Her body still trembled in the aftermath of Tony's anger. She knew that only her sex had prevented Tony from punching her in the mouth.

What was there about him that pushed her into stepping over the boundaries of decent human behaviour? She had no right to goad him that way. He had no right to grab her and fondle her and kiss her whenever he felt like it, either, she told herself. And, what was worse, to assume that she enjoyed it. Just because he was the great and god-like Tony Hart, the irresistible hero... He toyed with her. Kissed her when he felt like it, stopped when he felt like it. What about her feelings? Didn't he care that he was shredding her emotions to rags?

This was all just another game to him. In a few days or weeks, speculation about them would have died away and he would go out of her life. Raising her to heights of great passion, and then dashing her down on the hard rock of reality. He didn't care about her. Hadn't he told her often enough that he didn't intend to care about any woman? Hero-worship and adulation had been part of his life for so long that he expected every woman he met to fall for him. He probably thought that Erin was grateful for the few crumbs that he had dropped from his banquet table. Now he would know how grateful she was. And why.

Erin slowly unscrewed the lid from the bottle of flux. Guiltily she remembered the incredulous look on Tony's face at her brazen inquisition, his scorching anger at the realisation that Tony Hart, the fabled user of women, was himself being used.

Her hands shook, spilling the flux on the window before her. Tony's window. He would have to come back for his window. He had better. He hadn't paid for it yet. No. Tony hadn't paid the price. Erin was the one paying the price. She squeezed her eyelids tightly together in a futile attempt to hold back the flood of tears that threatened.

At least if Tony never came back for his window he would never know that Erin had lied to him. Going into his arms had nothing to do with learning skills. It had everything to do with something else. Using the cuff of her shirtsleeve, Erin wiped the warm tears from her face. Weeping was as pointless as trying to determine just when she had fallen in love with Tony. It might have been when he had first smiled at her from across the room at Merry's house, or maybe when she'd felt his pride as he had exhibited his beautifully crafted wood work, or even when he'd laughed at her as she had reacted to his hot chilli. More than likely it was an accumulation of all those things—and more. She had been in the habit of disliking him for so long, that she hadn't even noticed love creeping up on her. How could she have been so blind to the way her heart leapt at the sound of a whistled tune, the way her blood raced at the sight of his car in the driveway, and the way she had trouble breathing when he stood too close to her? Even the way she desperately sought to escape his presence should have warned her.

Well, it was all over now. Not that there had ever been anything to be over. Tony had said from the beginning he wasn't interested in her. No, he had said he wasn't interested in a girl like her. Erin toyed with the roll of copper foil. Would Tony be interested in her if she weren't a girl like her? Was virginity as important to her as losing Tony? What a stupid question. Tony had never been hers to lose. He wanted her, but only on terms of his choosing. Temporary terms. Tony didn't love her now, but at least he respected her. If she threw that away, she would have nothing. Besides, if parting with Tony hurt now, how much more unendurable it would be if she had experienced the fullness of his love.

Erin looked down at the window before her. Tony would soon walk away from her and the two of them would go their separate ways. Tony's life would always be filled with women. So many that he wouldn't remember their names, even the ones he slept with. Except for one. Every morning when the sun shone in, a rainbow of colours would silently steal forth from this window over to Tony's bed and kiss him awake.

Erin plugged in her soldering iron. This window would be the best she had ever made. Tony Hart was not going to be able to forget her even if he wanted to. Every time he made love to another woman in his bedroom, when he awoke the next morning, this window, her window, would be there to remind him of Erin Cassidy. She pushed away the unwelcome thought that perhaps Tony wouldn't even want the window now.

CHAPTER EIGHT

WORKING on Tony's window became an obsession with Erin. Long hours over her work bench left her back and shoulders aching and her eyes rimmed in red from the soldering fumes. But now the window was almost complete. Wearily Erin pushed the headscarf further back from her forehead. The movement drew her attention to the red, raw burn on her left hand where she had inadvertently touched it with her hot soldering gun. Her right hand was stiff from the hours of intense work and she slowly flexed her fingers. All the window needed now was cleaning. She carefully inspected her soldering job. There were no bubbles or peaks, no rough edges or uneven lines. The work was flawless. She slumped wearily on her stool. The stained-glass piece was too large to clean in her workshop sink. She would need to wash it outside using a picnic table and the hose. She looked out of her workshop window. It was later than she had realised; dusk had already fallen. It was too dark to wash the window tonight. Tomorrow. And then she would call Tony.

He was abrupt on the phone. She would have to bring the window out to his house. He was in the middle of fitting a cabinet into one of the bathrooms. About to point out that she didn't deliver, Erin swallowed her words. She did want to see the window in the bedroom; besides, she might as well be honest with herself. This might be her last opportunity to see Tony. He had been noticeably absent from the Cassidy household since Erin had informed him that she only kissed him because of what she could learn from him. Coming to her house, getting the window, putting it in his car— he would be gone in a matter of minutes. If she went to his house, at the very least good manners would impel him to offer her something to drink. She would have the chance to store up memories of him in the surroundings that she loved best, amidst his own beautifully crafted work.

Slowed down by the inevitable highway construction as she drove down Parker Road, Erin's palms were sweaty with anticipation. The day was sunny, the sky a blueberry pie decorated with whipped-cream clouds, the mountains to the west a lavender smudge above the horizon. Closer at hand, the roadside was apple-green, a legacy of the April blizzard with its life-giving moisture. The many cars parked at the nurseries and greenhouses along the west side of the road testified to the arrival of the planting season in local gardens. Through her open car window the swooshing of passing cars alternated with the melodic singing from meadowlarks perched on fence posts. In the distance the snow-covered summit of Pikes Peak looked like a low-hanging cloud. A hawk circled a small pasture, and Erin empathised with the hapless creature on the ground who was no doubt paralysed with fear and indecision.

Erin pulled into the driveway of Tony's house, and sat there in the car for a moment trying to collect her emotions. It wouldn't do to let Tony know how she was dreading seeing him and looking forward to it all at the same time. With the delivery of this window, a chapter in her life would come to a close. She blinked sudden tears from her eyes. Tony had angered her, he had entertained her, he had surprised her, scolded her, confused her, praised her, dismayed her...and worst of all, made her fall in love with him. And now, after today, they would part. The only thing that Tony Hart had wanted from her she was bringing him right now. A window. There was only one other thing that she could give him. Her love. And he didn't want that. She sighed, and stepped out of the car.

'Come on in. The door's open,' Tony's voice hollered from somewhere in the house when she rang the doorbell.

Erin opened the door and peeked inside. Tony was nowhere to be seen. 'I need some help,' she called. 'Could you hold the door open while I bring in the window?'

The top half of Tony's body appeared over the half-wall that edged the upstairs portion of the house. 'Be there in a second. Let me make sure the path is clear to the bedroom.' His head disappeared.

Erin returned to the car and opened the rear hatch of the station wagon. She had used her father's car so that the window could lie flat. A sheet of foam had protected the glass from damage as she drove, and Erin was relieved to see that the window had survived the journey without damage.

'Let me carry it.' Tony had quietly arrived. 'You hold the door. Any particular way I need to handle this?'

'Just carefully, even though the copper foil and solder give it strength. Watch out for that protrusion on the car,' she cautioned as Tony picked up the window. Running ahead of him, she held the front door open as he manoeuvred the heavy glass through. She was on his heels as he went slowly up the stairs and deposited the window on a makeshift workbench of boards laid across saw horses.

'Whew. That's heavier than I expected.' Walking over to the corner, he picked up a polished wooden circle. 'Here's the frame. What do you think?' He held it above the stained glass.

'I think it will look super,' Erin said, even as she thought, *he hasn't looked at me, really looked at me, yet.* Gingerly she reached out and stroked the dark, gleaming surface. 'What kind of wood is it?' *There had to be more than this. How could she get him to look at her? To really talk to her?*

'Walnut. Did you bring your bill?' he asked, in an abrupt change of subject.

'Y...yes.' *He was anxious for her to leave,* she thought in dismay. *There was no way to prolong her stay without his discovering her secret.* The bill was in her pocket, and she dug it out and handed it to him.

Tony's hand closed over hers, crushing the bill between them.

Erin caught her breath at the look of hostility which blanketed his face. *Tony had neither forgotten nor forgiven her words of the other day.*

'Wouldn't you like another lesson in lovemaking techniques before you go?' he asked savagely.

Heart thudding beneath her blouse, Erin quickly shook her head. 'No, no, I don't need one.'

'That's where you're wrong.' His hand twisted her arm behind her, thrusting her body up hard against his. 'You still have a lot to learn.' His lips twisted ironically. 'And as you pointed out, I'm the master.'

Erin squeezed her eyelids tightly closed, shutting out twin flames that burned in dark blue eyes. Tony chuckled softly, a demoniacal sound that sent nervous shivers down her spine. He buried his free hand in her hair, forcing her head up. His skin burned hers where they touched. Her mind raced in erratic circles, frantically issuing orders to limbs too weak to obey. This wasn't what she wanted, not to be kissed in anger. His embrace meant nothing. He was only doing this to punish her. He captured her mouth in a deep kiss that conquered any lingering resistance to being in his arms. The past and the future didn't matter. Only the present was important. Uppermost in her mind was the thought, one last kiss, what could it hurt?

His mouth softened against hers, moving persuasively to part her lips. She could not deny him. In the background a radio was playing, a singer crooning about the pain of love. Tony's large palms cradled her face, holding it immobile as he lingeringly explored her mouth. When he would have abandoned it, she gingerly caught his tongue between her teeth, letting him know that she, too, wanted to explore. He tasted of mint.

His hands slid slowly down her neck, the toughened palms exacerbating nerve-endings already trembling beneath his touch. One thumb pressed softly against the pulse at the base of her neck, causing it to throb, the beat echoing in her ears. Twisting her head, she sought the warmth and comfort of his neck, inhaling deeply the tang of aftershave overlaid on the scent of his skin. Her hands crept up to comb through the silken waves of his hair, and she nibbled on his ear-lobe, then bathed the tender red tip lightly with her tongue. One hand cradling her hips, Tony shifted her within his embrace, allowing him access to the buttons down the front of her blouse. One by one he slipped the buttons from the buttonholes, his movements so agonisingly deliberate that Erin wanted to scream with frustration. At last her blouse hung free and open, and Tony slid it slowly off her shoulders. Erin shivered as Tony's calloused fingertips trailed down her shoulders and chest to the front of her bra. The lacy garment was quickly disposed of. The air seemed frigid against her heated skin, and she burrowed into Tony's arms seeking warmth and sanctuary from the sudden embarrassment she felt at finding herself half-naked in his embrace.

Without a word he picked her up and carried her to his bed where he laid her on top of the covers before dropping down on top of her. Her gaze dropped before the disturbing light in his eyes, the cleft in his chin catching her attention. Like a small kitten, she reached up with her tongue and lapped at the dent. A half-day's growth of whiskers rasped against her tongue. His body was warm and heavy the length of hers. She slid her hands beneath his T-shirt, thrilled by the feel of his warm, sinewy back. His body was tense, the muscles clenched under her touch. Pushing him away from her, she tugged on his shirt until he pulled it over his head and tossed it to the floor. His chest was warm against her naked breasts, and she kneaded the muscles of his back until she felt some of the rigidity leave them. His hands were busy, exploring, teasing, warming, caressing until Erin was moaning with pleasure. She didn't feel him undo the zip on her jeans, but suddenly one large palm was centered on her stomach, stirring unfamiliar, hot sensations deep inside her. Tony's legs parted hers, and his hand slowly massaged her stomach.

'How do you like your lesson so far?' Tony whispered huskily.

Erin stiffened in horror. Tony was deliberately seducing her to teach her a lesson. And not a lesson in making love. He intended that she learn that Tony Hart was not a man to be trifled with. She tried to shove him off her body, but he only chuckled at her puny efforts. 'Please, Tony,' she choked.

'Please what?' he asked in a harsh voice. 'Please make love to me, Tony?' He tugged on the waistband of her jeans, lowering them a couple of inches.

Erin struggled to pull them up, but he captured her hands, holding them both in one of his. Her legs were still pinned beneath his lower body, but he shifted just enough to expose her nude torso to his view. She squeezed her eyes shut to prevent tears of frustration from escaping as his free hand roamed leisurely over her body. A finger traced the top of her jeans sending quivers across her stomach. Her humiliation was complete when she felt her breasts swelling at his touch, the nipples hardening at the insistence of his roving fingers.

'Is the class too advanced for you?' Tony's voice was full of mockery. 'That's just too bad, because as you so accurately pointed out the other day, my dealings with you have drastically curtailed my love-life. Surely you want to rectify that.' His hand continued to roam at will across her body.

She lay passive, refusing to resist, sensing that Tony wanted her to fight him, to push him into a course of action that she knew instinctively would destroy him. Her words the other day had hurt him, and he was seeking revenge. She sought to make amends. 'I didn't mean what I said the other day. I'm sorry if I upset you.'

'I'll bet you are,' he said savagely. 'Unfortunately for you, your retraction comes a little late. Because, you see, my needs haven't been met lately.' He spat out the words from between clenched teeth, before lowering his head.

She wouldn't fight him. He was only trying to scare her. He wouldn't really carry out his implied intentions. He was panting, his breath coming in warm bursts against her cheek. 'You'd like to help me out, wouldn't you, Erin? You and your honeyed lips, provocative breasts and soft, rounded belly.'

Erin willed herself not to respond, but the erotic words and sensual stroking of his hand continued to inflame her senses. She loved Tony so much. She couldn't let him take her by force; he would hate himself for ever. She gambled on the truth. 'I won't let you rape me, Tony. That would end up hurting you as much as me. I don't want you to continue this, but if you feel you must, I won't fight you. All I'm going to ask is . . . please remember that I'm a . . . that it's my first time . . . and . . . be gentle . . .' Her voice died away to a whisper. 'Please.'

Tony's body stiffened, his hand clenched convulsively around one swollen breast. Erin was afraid even to breathe for fear she would tip the odds the wrong way. Tony released her hands and rolled off the bed. 'Get dressed,' he ordered harshly. 'I'll be in the kitchen. I want to talk to you before you leave.' Picking up his shirt from the floor, he left the room without once looking at her.

Erin lay on the bed, drained of all feeling and emotion. She had won. No. Tony's better self had won. She rolled over limply and sat up. Her blouse and bra lay across the room. She wasn't sure she had the strength to pick them up and put them on.

Tony was waiting for her in the kitchen. He wouldn't wait long. She forced herself to move.

Her footsteps sounded like claps of thunder as she tiptoed down the uncarpeted stairs, carrying her shoes in her hands. Talking to Tony now was the last thing she wanted to do. Her only chance was to sneak out of the front door before he realised she wasn't still up in his bedroom. She looked towards the kitchen, straining to hear any sound that would tell her where he was.

He was leaning against the front door, his tall, muscular body blocking her escape. 'Going somewhere?' he asked tightly.

'Home.' Erin stuck out her chin, defying him to stop her.

Of course he did, grabbing her arm and pulling her out into the kitchen where he shoved her unceremoniously down on a chair and thrust a glass of iced tea on the table in front of her. The civilities over, he stalked over to the french doors overlooking the golf course, and stood, his back to her. 'We'll have to get married,' he said without preliminaries.

'What?' Erin choked on the tea.

After checking over his shoulder that she was all right, he once again faced the outdoors. 'Don't act so surprised. We both know that's been your aim all along.'

'Has it?' Erin breathed, the fury in her starting to build up. 'I think someone forgot to tell me that.'

Tony turned around and faced her, waving his arm wearily, his face so unhappy that Erin almost softened. 'Never mind. After what happened up there, I have no choice.'

'Nothing happened,' Erin cried.

Tony snorted. 'That's your idea of nothing?'

'You know what I mean. It isn't like, we, uh, well, you know. We both lost control, that's all.'

'That's not all, and you know it. I would have, I wanted to.'

'But you didn't,' Erin protested furiously. 'That's what counts.'

'You think that's how your parents would feel if they'd seen us, writhing half-naked on the bed? Your dad would have turned his shotgun on me,' he said bitterly.

'My dad doesn't have a shotgun,' Erin said, trying to lighten the tension.

Tony brushed her levity aside. 'I could never face him again, trying to rape his daughter.'

Erin had had about enough of Tony's breast-beating. If he thought for one minute that she was going to marry him just because he felt guilty about what he had done, he was crazy. Maybe her secret desire was to spend the rest of her life in Tony's arms, but not this way. Fighting the married state as fiercely as he had, he would resent their marriage the rest of his life. No matter that the whole idea was his. It wouldn't be long before he had twisted it in his mind so that Erin was to blame for the whole mess. Well, she wasn't having any of it. She shoved back the kitchen chair and stood up. 'Whether you can ever face my father again is your problem, not mine, and I have no intention of marrying you so you can solve it. I wouldn't marry you if you were the last man on earth,' she added furiously. How dare he think she would marry a man for reasons other than love? She turned to leave.

'You'd better take me up on my offer now, because it's your last chance. I won't ask you again,' Tony warned.

She slammed the front door as she went out. There. That should answer him. She never wanted to see him again.

Unfortunately she reckoned without her youngest brother. Nicky dropped the bomb casually at dinner a couple of nights later. 'Tony said that Sunday is OK with him.'

Erin looked at him in shock. 'OK for what?'

'The art museum. You're the one who insisted that I needed to expand my horizons. Of course,' he went on hopefully, 'if you've changed your mind . . .'

'I haven't.' Erin carefully chose her words, feeling as though she were picking her way through a mine-field. 'I'm just surprised that Tony is planning to go with us.' She tried not to read any significance in this unexpected development, but a tiny flicker of hope refused to die out.

'He said he would, didn't he? Tony wouldn't go back on his word,' Nicky said with assurance.

'I suppose not.' Was Tony using the excursion as an excuse to see her again?

The day of the museum outing turned out to be a sunny Colorado spring day. Hearing Tony's deep voice from downstairs, Erin checked her appearance in the mirror. She had dressed with special care. A white linen blouse, its V-neck trimmed in white embroidery, topped a full dirndl cotton skirt, the royal blue fabric splashed with cabbage roses in vivid shades of red and burgundy. A dark, fat braid hung over one shoulder, its end secured with a bright red ribbon. A single silver chain encircled her slender neck and red painted toenails peeked out from matching red sandals. She grabbed up a red bag and nervously went down the stairs.

Tony was in the living-room talking to her parents and Nicky. Her younger brother had honoured the occasion by donning slacks in place of the ubiquitous flowered shorts that were the teenager uniform this spring. Erin avoided looking directly at Tony but every sense screamed to her of his presence. The shirt that moulded his muscular chest was in the shade of blue that he frequently wore. No doubt one of his many girlfriends had told him that it matched his eyes, and it suited his vanity to wear it often.

Outside, she quickly jumped into the back seat of Tony's small station wagon, leaving the front passenger seat free for Nicky. Neither male bothered to object. They sat in the front seat discussing sports all the way downtown. Erin sat in the back, torn between annoyance and self-pity. Why in the world were they bothering to take her if they intended to ignore her? She pretended a great interest in the traffic around them on Colfax Avenue, arousing from her apathy only when she realised that Tony was turning in the wrong direction. 'I thought we were going to the Denver Art Museum.'

Tony didn't bother to turn his head. 'I thought that Nicky might find the Museum of Western Art more enjoyable.'

Erin glared at the back of his head. 'You might have discussed it with me before deciding.'

'Discussed it? Or argued about it? By making the decision, I saved us having to fight about it.'

Erin flounced back against the car seat. He was the most arbitrary, inconsiderate person she had ever met. She would certainly never admit to him that he was probably correct in thinking Nicky would prefer the western art. The collection was smaller than the one owned by the more formal museum, but displayed in a thoughtful, pleasing manner. Secretly Erin loved the museum, located in the Navarre, an old brick building that had housed one of Denver's fanciest brothels in days gone by. An underground tunnel had led from the Navarre to the Brown Palace Hotel to allow the rich and famous who stayed in one to secretly visit the other. The Brown Palace also still stood, an Italian Renaissance grand lady who snubbed her nose at the modern buildings that towered above her less pretentious neighbour across the street.

They started their viewing on the third floor. 'I was surprised when Nicky said you were coming,' Erin said coolly to Tony as they stood before a Russell bronze.

'After my pep-talk to him the other day, I felt a certain responsibility.'

'Of course, I know how you feel about carrying out your responsibilities,' she goaded him, all hope that he had arranged the outing as an excuse to see her draining away.

He raised his eyebrows.

His silence irritated her, egging her on to evoke some emotion from him. 'After all, you did seem to feel that you owed me a marriage proposal after your behaviour the other day.'

'After thinking about the situation, I decided that you were right. My attitude was too Victorian for today. So many people are hopping in and out of various beds, our little escapade hardly merits even remembering,' he said, in a bored tone of voice, moving on to study a Bierstadt landscape.

'I'm sure that's true for you,' Erin hissed angrily. 'It was just one more incident of sleaze in a life filled with . . .'

Tony turned to her with such rage on his face that she bit off the rest of her sentence and moved across the room with indecent speed to stand at Nicky's side.

Tony leisurely joined them. As they browsed their way down each level of the museum, it soon became clear that although Tony had not been trained in art appreciation and his knowledge was spotty, he approached art with a natural appreciation and insight. Erin was annoyed at finding him comfortable in her private domain. Her irritation was not lessened by Nicky hanging on to Tony's every word.

Perhaps if Tony had somehow conceded her superior knowledge, Erin wouldn't have embarked on a course that ruined the afternoon for everyone. When they both admired a mountain landscape, she had been contemptuous, sneeringly referring to it as calendar art. She corrected Tony's assumptions, disparaged his opinions and ridiculed his observations.

Nicky grew more and more silent as they walked through the museum, darting sideways looks of puzzlement and disbelief at Erin as she interrupted Tony with condescending remarks interspersed with esoteric explanations designed to underline his ignorance.

The last painting they came to was a Jackson Pollock. Nicky and Tony were united in their dislike of it. Although Erin was not a fan of the artist, she immediately took exception to their judgement, saying in a patronising voice, 'Of course, it takes knowledge to appreciate art such as this. People of discernment and good taste would be thrilled to hang a Pollock in their living-room.'

Tony shrugged. 'I have one in my garage.'

'You have a Jackson Pollock in your garage?' Erin repeated in disbelief.

'A facsimile, actually. I call it a drip cloth.'

'A drip cloth?'

'When I paint, I put it under my ladder to catch all the drips. I'm a pretty messy painter, so it looks just like this so-called masterpiece.' Tony winked at Nicky who snickered in response.

'Don't tell me. Let me guess. You're one of those people who brag that they don't know art, but they do know what they like,' Erin said contemptuously.

'I've had enough. I'll be in the car when you finish.' Tony walked to the door.

Nicky refused to look at Erin. 'I'll come with you.'

Ashamed of her behaviour, yet incapable of apologising, Erin trailed behind the two to Tony's car. How could she have behaved so badly? A squirrel sitting cockily on a dustbin, the colourful beds of iris in the Civic Center, the gaggle of tourists posing beneath the gold-domed Capitol building on the step that denoted they were exactly one mile above sea level—small scenes that normally brought a smile to her face—all failed to disperse her misery and self-pity. She didn't blame Tony and Nicky for totally ignoring her presence as they headed home.

Tony slammed on the brakes in the Cassidy driveway and stared straight ahead, a set look on his face. Nicky gave him a shame-faced look. 'I don't suppose you want to come in for a while.'

'No,' Tony spat out. Then seeing the chagrined look on the teenager's face, he reached over and lightly cuffed him on the arm. 'I'll be in touch.'

'Sure.' His shoulders slumped in dejection, Nicky walked into the house.

Erin panicked. Her seat-belt was stuck or she would never have let Nicky go in without her. Cravenly she admitted her willingness to hide behind her younger brother. Struggling with the belt, she looked up. Tony was watching her in the rear-view mirror, contempt so clearly written on his face, that Erin felt herself blushing with shame.

'Thanks for a very revealing day,' he said, tight-lipped. 'The next time I think about doing something as stupid as this, I'll stick my head in a meat-grinder instead. That would be more fun.' Seeing Erin still having trouble with the refractory belt, he swore viciously before leaning over the front seat and jerking it loose.

She opened her mouth to thank him, to apologise, to say anything, but the words withered before the savage look on his face. Hiding her shame behind a shield of ice, she stepped haughtily from his car. He barely waited until she had shut the car door before he thrust the car into gear and roared out of the driveway. Erin jumped as spitting gravel in the wake of his departure stung her bare legs.

Slowly she moved towards the house, dreading the comments that Nicky was sure to make. He stepped out on to the porch, watching her as he ripped the top off a can of fizzy drink. 'I suppose that you're going to tell me that I'm too young to understand,' he said, his voice cracking as it still did when he was under stress.

He looked so unhappy and defenceless standing there, waiting to hear his sister tell him that there was a good reason for what he had endured today. The only problem was, there wasn't a good reason. Erin closed her eyes and bit her lower lip. She didn't want the horrible afternoon to come between them.

She had to say something. In the end she merely apologised for ruining his day.

He nodded his head in acknowledgement. 'I guess you and Tony must have had a big fight. I wondered why he seemed surprised when I called him about going today. I suppose that means your engagement is off.'

'It was never on. You know that Tony and I were just pretending to be...to be serious about each other because of the newspaper articles. There was never anything to it.'

'I know that's what you said,' Nicky said enigmatically. He took a sip of his drink before exploding into speech. 'Jeez, Erin, no wonder Tony never asked you to marry him. I couldn't believe the way you treated him today.'

Stung by his remark, Erin spoke without thinking. 'For your information, he proposed and I turned him down.'

'For crying out loud. You turned him down? Are you nuts or something? Erin, you're not going to cry, are you?'

Erin managed to conjure up a watery smile. 'No, I'm not going to cry,' she assured her brother as she walked up the steps and sat down in the porch swing.

Nicky was not totally convinced. He dropped into the swing beside her and awkwardly patted her on the shoulder. 'Want to talk about it?'

'There's nothing to talk about. Tony and I have never liked each other much, and now that the talk about his alibi has died away, there's no need to pretend any more.'

'Come on, Erin. A blind man could tell that you're crazy about Tony.'

She sniffed, refusing to concede anything. 'It doesn't matter. Tony never wanted to marry me.'

'Sure he didn't. That's why he asked you.'

'He...he only asked...something happened...he thought... Oh, what does it matter?' she asked wearily. 'The bottom line is that Tony doesn't love me, he never has...' She hiccuped on a sob. 'He doesn't even like me.'

Nicky scrunched up his face thoughtfully. 'Tony has been hanging around this house ever since he met you,' he said at last.

'Not because of me. He likes the rest of you. You're his friends.'

'Tony has lots of friends,' Nicky pointed out drily. 'Why doesn't he eat Sunday dinner with them every week? I can't believe he wasn't asked. And don't tell me it's because of Mom's apple pie,' he forestalled her explanation. 'What is it Tony's always saying? He studies the opposition, does his homework and then figures out his game plan. I kinda thought that was what he was doing hanging around here all the time. Now let me finish,' he cut Erin off again. 'Think about it a little. You told me about him following you home after that party. And didn't he jump right in and deck Martin after that creep slugged you? You may think I'm just a kid, but it seemed to me that Tony came to your rescue awful quick after that stuff came out in the papers.'

'He felt obliged to. He didn't like it. If you could have seen how mad he was at me for having to do it.'

'Mad at you? Or mad that someone he cared about was in a fix, and he blamed himself?'

'Oh, what difference does it make?' Erin asked wearily. 'I'll never see Tony again after today anyway.'

'You could call him up and apologise for the way you acted today.'

Tears flooded Erin's eyes. 'It's more than just that.'

'Then what?'

'It's, oh, you wouldn't understand, Nicky.'

Nicky stood up, crushing the empty can in his hands. 'I knew we'd get to the "you're too young too understand" bit. Maybe I am, but I do know one thing. This love business is sure stupid. A blind man can see that you and Tony are crazy in love with each other. I'm never going to fall for some girl and get myself tied up in knots like you two are.' Shaking his head in disgust, he disappeared into the house.

CHAPTER NINE

LEAVING behind his thoroughly miserable sister. Erin slowly swung back and forth in the swing, Nicky's parting words ringing in her ears. He was right about one thing. Tony had certainly tied her up into knots. She just wished she could believe Nicky was right about Tony's motives, but she knew better. Tony had let her know from the very beginning that he was interested in her only as a temporary playmate. No doubt if she had willingly warmed his bed in the beginning he would have long ago moved on. That was her mistake. She should have pursued him until he had run from her in panic. Instead her lack of interest had challenged him. He had brought all his considerable weapons to bear in charming her out of her dislike of what he stood for—a playboy and an athlete. Succeeding all too well. How he would laugh if he knew that the Erin Cassidy who had coolly informed him at Merry's party that she wasn't interested in football players had gone and fallen in love with one.

Laugh? No, Tony wouldn't laugh. He would run as far and as fast as he could. As he had told Erin too many times, love and marriage weren't on his agenda. She could almost feel sorry for him. Had his father ever realised what he had done to his son? Poor Tony. The teenage years were such fragile ones. Caught between wanting to be a man, and reluctant to leave the security of childhood, he must have been devastated by his father's revelations. The scars were well hidden, but none the less, they existed. Erin wondered if Tony realised that his own aversion to marriage could probably be traced back to his father's indiscretions. The woman who could convince Tony that marital infidelity was not inherited would be a lucky woman indeed. It wasn't marriage that Tony was running from; it was the fear of failure.

Apparently Nicky discussed the situation with their parents, because from then on there was a conspiracy of silence on the subject of Tony Hart in the Cassidy household. If any of the others spoke with Tony, that fact was not mentioned to Erin. Nor was she surprised that Tony was notably absent from their house. Another crisis in the sports world had removed Tony's affairs from the sports pages, and even the gossip columns had found juicier meat for them to feast on. The supposed engagement between Tony Hart and Erin Cassidy was allowed to die a natural death. Erin was the only mourner.

Life had returned to its pre-Tony state of being, Erin told herself as she worked in her studio. Not exactly the same, of course. Martin was out of the picture. Business had picked up, thanks to Merry's enthusiastic sponsorship. She was doing just fine. Tony Hart was out of her life, but so what? She had managed without him before and she could do it again. Her life was full, happy, busy... A drop of salty water fell on the paper tacked to her drawing-board, and she brushed it aside.

The trouble was, Tony wasn't out of her life. The cheque for his window, arriving the day after their trip to the art museum, had provoked images of the hand that wrote it, the hand that was so capable on the gear lever, so tender against her breast. In spite of herself, she had watched an interview of Tony on TV where he had given the reporter a tour of his home, pausing to show off Erin's window, commenting on what a fine artist she was. She had had eyes only for his bed, remembering the way his bare skin had felt against hers. Calls came regularly from friends and neighbours of Tony's, all interested in commissioning stained glass, all referred by him. She told herself that she owed him no gratitude, that her work stood on its own merit.

The window she was working on now was the team logo of the Explorers football team, commissioned by the management of the team to go in their offices. The man who had ordered it was a sharp, articulate businessman, further destroying her illusions that those associated with the sport of football were borderline illiterates. Tony would have mocked the surprise on her face when she had seen the man's tastefully decorated office, the impressive art that decorated the walls.

Erin laid down her pattern scissors. When would she ever stop thinking constantly about Tony? Would the ache deep within her ever go away? She found herself listening hopefully for footsteps bounding up the stairs two at a time, listening for the roar of an expensive sports car, listening for his light-hearted whistling of old Irish tunes. Working in her shop, a smell or a sound would trigger a painful association and she would sit, her work forgotten, lost in memory. The nights were the worst. The June breezes would creep through her open bedroom window, swaying the lace curtains and carrying an elusive scent of roses that instantly transported Erin back to her workshop and into Tony's arms.

'Erin!'

Nicky's yell brought her abruptly out of her reverie. 'I'm up here,' she shouted back.

Nicky ran thunderously up the outside staircase and stuck his head into her workshop. 'You listening to the radio?'

'No, why.'

'Just wondered if you heard about Tony.'

Erin shot off her stool. 'What about Tony?'

'According to the radio he got hurt today at the Explorers' minicamp.'

'Hurt? How bad?'

'Don't know. He's not in the hospital, but that doesn't mean much.' He fiddled with Erin's scissors. 'I hope this doesn't mean the end of his football career. I don't think the Explorers can make the play-offs without him.'

'I'd have thought you'd be more interested in Tony's condition than some stupid game,' Erin said tightly. 'I thought he was your friend.'

Nicky shrugged. 'Yeah, well, you're my sister.'

'Oh, Nicky,' Erin cried, 'I don't want you to feel that you have to choose between us. Just because Tony and I aren't right for each other doesn't make Tony less of a good person. I want you to stay his friend.'

'Maybe you're right. He'll probably need all the friends he can get now.'

'What do you mean?'

'Hey, it's one thing to be friends with a football hero, it's another to be friends with a football has-been.'

'Nicky!' Erin was appalled by his brother's assessment.

'You'll see,' he said darkly before disappearing down the stairs.

Erin dropped weakly back on to her stool. Tony hurt! It couldn't be. He worked out daily, he was so strong, in such good shape. How would he feel if he couldn't play football again? A football has-been, Nicky called him. No, not Tony. Maybe he wouldn't be able to play a silly game any more, but Tony would never be a has-been. He had too many talents, too much ambition to count in this world. Surely all his friends knew that and would refuse to abandon him. She gnawed on the inside of her cheek. If only she could be sure that Tony wasn't alone right now. What if he needed a friend right now? He wouldn't call Erin. He didn't consider her a friend.

She slumped against the work bench, her mind racing. Did she have the courage to go out to Tony's house? She loved him. What if he thought she had only come because she thought that he was through with football? He wouldn't welcome pity. What if he wasn't through with football? Nicky might have misunderstood the severity of Tony's injury. Did she care? Tony was Tony, whether he played football, built furniture or dug ditches. What he did wasn't nearly as important as how he did it. Her mouth curved up in a slight smile. How he played the game, as Tony would say. Of course, all that was irrelevant. She had long ago faced up to the fact that she loved Tony no matter what he did.

The problem was, Tony didn't love her. Even if everyone thought he did. Erin sat bolt upright. Why did everyone think Tony loved her? In spite of all her protestations to the contrary, her entire family had persisted in treating their sham engagement as if it were the real thing. There had been no doubt in their minds that Tony and she were in love. Of course, they had not heard Tony proclaim time and time again that he had no intention of getting married. She had. Slowly she examined that thought from all directions. Had she been so busy listening to what Tony said that she had missed how Tony felt? There had been no reason for him to propose to her that day at his house. Could it be that Tony wanted to marry her but was so afraid of it that he had put himself in a position where he would be forced to do so?

Erin stood up. She could hole up here in her workshop sitting passively while life and Tony passed her by, or she could take matters into her own hands. Tony had told her he would never ask her to marry him again. He hadn't said that she couldn't ask him. On the way to the house, she made her plans, a silly, hopeful grin plastered across her face.

'Nicky!' Erin hollered as she ran into the house. 'Where are you?'

Her brother came down the hall from the kitchen. 'Here. What's up?'

'Has Mike Francis found a new home for his dog yet?'

'No, and he's getting worried. They're not moving until July, but he wants to make sure that Joe has a good home. He won't settle for just anyone.' He looked unhappy. 'I wish I weren't allergic to dogs so I could take him. He's a great dog.'

'Nicky, do you think that Mike would let me have the dog?'

'I suppose, but you can't have a dog when you're living here. You know what the doctor said about me and dog hair. I just keep wheezing and can't get my breath. He said I might outgrow it, but I don't think I'm going to by July.'

'The truth is, I don't want the dog for myself. I thought that I might give him to Tony.' She avoided looking in her brother's direction.

'That's a dumb idea. How can Tony take care of a dog when he's gone so much during the season?'

'He could if he had someone to take care of the dog for him.'

'And who's he going to get for that?'

'Me.'

'You? Even supposing that Tony would accept the dog from you, did you plan to drive clear down to Parker several times a day to feed and exercise him?'

'Actually,' Erin said carefully, concentrating on polishing the banister newel with her hand, 'I was planning on living a little closer than that.'

A big smile appeared on Nicky's face. 'I'll call Mike.'

An hour later, Erin looked in her rear-view mirror. 'I'm counting on you, Joe. Even if he wants to turn me down, he's bound to fall in love with you.'

The big red Irish setter responded with an enormous lopsided grin, his dark tongue hanging out of one side of his mouth, his ears blowing backwards in the draught from Erin's open window. As she drove through Parker, the bank clock registered six-thirty. Clumps of yellow sweet clover perfumed the air between clouds of diesel fumes. Down the street from Tony's house the mist from a sprinkler sported a rainbow of colours, while a robin bathed nearby in a small puddle. A phalanx of cow birds, their brown heads bobbing to an unseen martial melody, marched across a wide expanse of green lawn.

A blue Mercedes was parked in Tony's driveway. Tony had company. Her courage, never that strong to begin with, began to drain away, and she considered driving right on past. Two small boys playing in Tony's front yard saw her and immediately began shouting her name. She had no choice but to stop.

Adam and Davy Roberts backed away in awe as Erin snapped Joe's leash on him and led him from the car. The dog, intrigued with this new game, immediately stalked them. Davy ran shrieking into the house. Adam was persuaded to hold out a wavering hand. Joe slurped the hand all the way up to the child's face. By the time Neal Roberts appeared at Tony's front door, Adam was giggling with delight at his new friend.

Neal's eyes lit up. 'Erin. Come on in. And bring your friend. Or is he bringing you?' He laughed as the large dog bounded happily over to him, dragging Erin in his wake.

'Joe and I still have to vote on who's the boss,' she admitted breathlessly. Over Neal's shoulder she could see a tall, blonde woman walking towards the door. She recognised the woman immediately and her heart sank. 'I...I really can't come in,' she said hastily. 'I was just driving by and saw the boys.' Even to her own ears, the explanation sounded lame.

The blonde slipped between Neal and the open door. 'I heard Davy tell his father that a monster was outside with Erin, and I was curious.' Her lips curved in a friendly, infectious smile, compelling Erin to smile back. 'You must be Erin Cassidy. I recognise you from Tony's description. I'm Vicky Stephens.'

'I know. I saw your picture in the paper.' Erin felt as if the bottom had been ripped from her world. Tony didn't need her. Not when he could have this beautiful woman who radiated warmth and charm.

Vicky stepped back from the doorway. 'Come in.'

Erin held back. 'I really can't. I was just wondering how Tony was.'

'Come in and see for yourself,' Vicky insisted, grabbing Erin's arm and pulling her into the house. 'Look who's here,' she called out gaily.

Tony was sprawled on the sofa conversing with a tall, thin bespectacled man. At Vicky's announcement, he looked up. There was no hint of welcome in the cold face that stared at Erin. A huge silence filled the room. Erin wanted to crawl under the rug and hide. Her misery must have shown on her face, because everyone else immediately began talking at once.

Neal began asking questions about the dog, Merry offered her a drink, and Vicky said loudly, 'Erin, I'd like you to meet my fiancé, Jason Hughes. Jason, this is Tony's Erin.'

The thin man stretched out his hand to Erin. Thankfully she clasped his hand, murmuring the platitudes of new acquaintances, all the while her thoughts frantically tumbled about in her head. This man was going to marry Vicky Stephens. What about Tony? 'I didn't realise you were getting married,' Erin said cautiously.

'The first part of July,' Vicky explained. 'Jason can't take a honeymoon once the season starts.'

Erin looked in surprise at the thin man. She would never have guessed that he was a football player. He caught her look and laughed. 'I'm an orthopaedic surgeon,' he explained. 'I take care of Tony's million-dollar knees.'

Vicky smiled. 'Tony introduced Jason and me. That's why Jason trusts Tony to escort me around when he can't make it. And of course, Tony feels safe with me, since I'm engaged,' she added in a teasing voice.

Erin was more concerned about why an orthopaedic surgeon was at Tony's house now. 'My brother said he heard on the radio that Tony got hurt today.' Erin avoided looking at Tony.

'A slight ankle sprain. Nothing serious,' the doctor said in satisfaction.

Erin looked down at the glass of tea that Merry had handed her, unable to think of anything to say. She had been a fool to rush out here. Fortunately the two small boys provided a diversion. Adam had finally convinced Davy that Joe was harmless and the two of them were dissolved in giggles as they rolled on the floor with the dog. Tony narrowed his eyes thoughtfully at the sight of Joe.

'Where did this dog come from?' Merry demanded to know. 'He certainly is good with the children.'

'Right now he belongs to a friend of my brother's, but Mike's dad is in the service and the family is being transferred to England, so poor old Joe here can't go.' She risked a look in Tony's direction. He lay on the sofa, studying the ceiling as if he had never seen it before.

'The dog's name is Joe?' Neal asked in disbelief.

Erin nodded.

'Why such a plebeian name for such a beautiful dog?' Vicky asked.

'Joe was born during the '85 Super Bowl, so Mike, being an ardent football fan, named the puppy after one of the quarterbacks of that game.'

'Can Joe come live with us?' Adam teased his mother.

'Well,' said Merry thoughtfully, 'if he is looking for a home.' She raised her eyebrows at Erin.

Erin took a deep breath. 'Mike hopes... I told him... that is, he thinks he's already found a home for him.' That got Tony's attention. He gave Erin a quick glance from hooded eyes before snapping his fingers at the dog. Joe responded immediately, his tail waving in the air like a red flag.

A small smile hovered over Vicky Stephens' mouth. 'The perfect dog for you, Tony, with a name like that.'

The time had come to risk it all. Erin cleared her throat. 'Just what I thought. Mike has taught him to catch a football, and he swears that Joe will be the best receiver that Tony ever had.' A nerve-racking silence greeted her words.

'I think the dog agrees.' Neal nodded laughingly to the sofa where Tony lay with Joe's head resting on his knee.

'I don't see how in the world Tony can possibly keep a dog,' Merry said crossly.

Neal just laughed. 'Come on kids, wife. Time to head for home. Merry had to see for herself how you were, Tony.'

Vicky stood. 'We have to leave, too. Our dinner reservations are for seven-thirty. I'm glad your sprain is so minor, Tony.' She pulled a comical face. 'Daddy will be happy, too.'

Tony sat up, dislodging Joe's head. The dog looked at him with reproachful brown eyes. 'I appreciate everyone coming by.' He still didn't look at Erin.

Intense disappointment rolled over her. She fumbled for her handbag with blurry eyes. 'I'm parked behind you,' she said to Jason, her voice barely wavering.

Tony reached over and snatched the bag from her hands and dug in it until he found her car keys. He tossed the keys to Jason. 'Move Erin's car, will you? If she gets in it, she'll probably keep on going.'

Erin could feel her skin blush fiery red as everyone in the room turned to look at her. She stood up and held out her hand to Jason. 'May I have my car keys, please?'

'You don't have the nerve to play out the game, do you?' Tony taunted her, a challenging look in his deep azure eyes.

'A game,' she said bitterly. 'Everything is a game to you.' She glared at him, vaguely aware of the others filing out of the room and the front door softly closing.

Tony stood up, awkwardly, his weight on one foot. Immediately Erin was smitten with contrition. 'Tony, I'm sorry. Does it hurt badly?'

'No, it's fine.' He took a short step, wincing as he put weight on the sore ankle.

Erin shot to his side, a supporting arm tight around his waist.

'Maybe you could help me up to my bedroom before you leave,' he said weakly, grimacing with pain.

Instantly she forgot her anger, his arrogance. 'Of course.'

Leaning heavily on her shoulder, he limped towards the stairs. 'You'll be able to see how your window looks.'

'I saw it on television. Thank you for recommending me to so many of your friends,' she added politely.

At the last minute she remembered Joe and softly called to him to stay. The big red setter was lying on the floor. At her call he lifted his head and his large brown eyes seemed to rebuke her for her lack of courage. His watchful stance reminded her that Joe had a vested interest in her success. Taking a deep breath to give her courage, she resolutely marched Tony up the staircase.

His limp seemed to ease as she helped him across the room to his bed, and the small seed of suspicion within her grew larger. Tony lay down on the coverlet, his hands pillowing his head.

Erin sat gingerly on the edge of the bed. 'Nicky was really worried about your injury. He'll be happy to hear that it was so minor.'

'It was nice of him to be concerned. Don't tell him how painful it is. I wouldn't want him to worry about me,' he added plaintively.

Erin turned towards him. 'Nicky wasn't worried about you,' she said artlessly. 'He was worried about the Explorers' play-off chances.'

Tony looked at her sharply, taking in the innocent look on her face. 'When did you figure out that I was exaggerating the sprain?' he asked.

'I wondered when Jason didn't seem worried, and it seemed strange that pain would set in as soon as your doctor left. But the real giveaway was when you forgot to limp up the stairs.'

'Ah, I was afraid that you'd caught that.'

Erin took a deep breath. 'That's not the only thing that you've been afraid of lately.'

'Care to explain?' he asked ominously, propping his head up on one hand and studying her intently.

Erin's heart pounded beneath her ribs. 'You're scared of me.'

With deceptive speed one of Tony's arms snaked out and pulled Erin down on the bed beside him. Balancing on one elbow he brushed the hair back from her face and tucked it behind an ear. 'It takes more than a little squirt like you to scare me,' he said, his voice laced with mockery, as a lazy finger traced her cheekbone.

Erin's stomach dipped at his touch. She had to fight the impulse to bury her tongue in the cleft of his chin. 'Liar,' she said breathlessly, determined to have her say. 'You're afraid to admit that you love me, because then you might be tempted to marry me and you're afraid of marriage.'

'Assuming for argument's sake that you're right, do you mind telling me the reasoning you've dreamed up to support this fantasy of yours?'

She concentrated on his firm jawline. 'You told me once that my parents' marital situation was what they made of it, and that it wasn't any of my responsibility. Yet all these years, you've somehow assumed the burden of your father's guilt. Whatever his reasoning for his actions, infidelity is not hereditary. You are not destined to have a bad marriage just because your parents might have had. Besides...' Her courage almost faltered as she met his intense gaze.

'Besides, what?' he prodded.

She scowled at him. 'I'm going to leash you. Your tomcatting days are over.'

With one swift movement Tony rolled on top of her. 'You and who else?' he growled menacingly, his rugged face thrust close to her own.

She ignored the question. 'You said you'd never propose to me again, but you didn't say anything about me proposing to you.'

Tony's mouth hovered above hers. 'Am I to understand that you're asking me to marry you?'

'Yes. Please,' she added primly.

'You're crazy to risk it. What if I'm a failure at being a husband?'

'What if you're not? I'll take my chances. After five brothers, you think I can't handle you?' she teased.

'What a strange mixture you are,' Tony murmured. 'Innocent yet full of passion, the delicate beauty of a spring flower hiding the toughness of an old leather boot.' He dropped a swift kiss on her lips. 'Maybe that's why I love you so much.'

Erin's arms had somehow become wrapped around Tony's neck and now they tightened, holding him close to her. 'Do you really love me?' she asked wistfully.

'From the first time I saw you, I...no.' He shook his head in amusement. 'Not the first time. When I saw you at Merry's, playing with the boys. Your hair was messy, your nose shiny, and when I walked in you made no effort to fix or apologise for either. Helping out Merry, playing with the boys. That was important to you, not making an impression on someone like me. I thought then, I want the mother of my children to be that kind of a caring person. Then you smiled, tossed back your hair, and informed me you didn't like football players. How could I pass up a challenge like that?' He grinned ruefully. 'I admit I had no intention of falling in love with any woman, least of all one who couldn't stand football players. Sending you off alone to bed the night of the blizzard was one of the most difficult things I've ever done. That's when I began to suspect that I'd got in over my head with you.'

'And you blamed me,' Erin guessed. 'That's why you were in such a bad mood the next morning.'

'Guilty as charged. Then, when Martin slugged you . . .' He clamped his jaw tight on the memory. 'Of course Joanna guessed right away, and couldn't pass up the opportunity to tease me. I'd bragged too often at their house that no woman was ever going to domesticate me.'

Erin softly rubbed her cheek against him. 'No wonder you were so nasty to me after their party.'

'Nasty to you!' Tony said in a soft, explosive voice. 'Here I was so crazy with love for you that everyone could see it, and all you could talk about was how you wanted nothing to do with an athlete. I saw how bored you were watching that game on TV. It was as if you were trying to prove to me that we had absolutely nothing in common.'

Erin buried her head in his neck. 'I must have seemed so smug to you.' She raised her head and looked at him shyly. 'I didn't want to fall in love with you either. I thought it was just your experience that made me melt every time you came near.' Her hands kneaded the muscles that quivered beneath her touch. 'I even tried to tell myself that it was just your muscles I was crazy about. I was wrong about a lot of things. The kind of person you are, the kind of man I want to marry.' Her voice caught in her throat. 'I've been so unhappy without you.'

His mouth was tantalisingly close to Erin's, and before she had thought about what she was doing, her tongue darted out and traced the outline of his lips. 'You told me once that I was out of my league with you. You're wrong. I intend to be voted rookie of the year.'

'Who gets to vote?' Tony asked huskily.

Erin shifted on the bed, bringing her hips in closer contact with Tony's. 'Who do you think?' She closed her eyes, her pulse speeding up at the expression on Tony's face as his face lowered to hers.

Joe's cold nose shoving between them brought Erin back to her senses. 'I think he wants to go out,' she giggled, joy and happiness bubbling up inside her.

Tony grinned wryly back at her. 'And I suppose you're going to tell me that he's my dog so I have to get up and let him out.' Walking over to his cupboard, he pulled out a blue robe and handed it to Erin. 'Put this on before I forget that you want to be a virgin on your wedding night.'

Erin's breath caught in her throat. 'My wedding night?'

Tony pulled her up from the bed and wrapped the robe and his arms around her. 'Our wedding night,' he promised.

Standing at the french doors overlooking Tony's deck, they watched the large setter galloping around the back garden, stopping occasionally to investigate whatever caught his attention. Tony chuckled. 'You could have knocked me over with a feather when I looked up and saw you standing there with that damn dog. I couldn't figure out what in the world you were up to.' He gave her a lop-sided grin. 'Trust you to have a dog do your proposing for you.' He tightened his arms around her. 'At that, it was better than my proposal. I thought if I made it sound as if we had to get married, you wouldn't turn me down. I was sure that you'd rejected me because you thought we were too different. The trip to the museum was supposed to show you that we could share interests.' He snorted. 'It didn't go quite the way I intended. You blasted all my hopes. What made you show up here today?'

'Nicky,' she said simply. 'He couldn't understand why we were making such a mess of things when it was obvious to him that we were both in love. And then, my whole family kept acting as if our engagement were the real thing, as if it were the most natural thing in the world for you to love me.'

'Did you ever consider that maybe they're prejudiced?' Tony teased her.

'I know they are. They just want a quarterback in the family, and they're not any too particular about how they get him,' Erin retorted.

'And you? How do you feel about a quarterback in the family?'

'You're a person composed of many parts, Tony, and I love all those parts. Even football, because that's part of you, part of why you are the person you are, the person I love. I may never be the greatest football fan, but I'll always be *your* greatest fan.'

Tony's arms tightened around her. 'Weeks ago I warned you that the game wasn't over. It's over now and I won.'

Erin turned swiftly in his embrace. Her mouth close to his, she breathed, 'The game of love is never over and we're both winners.'

In disgust, Joe gave up scratching at the door and lay down on the grass, the Frisbee he had found cradled between his paws. Didn't these humans ever play games?

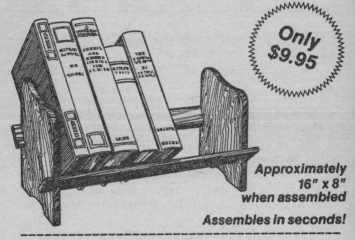